RDF

0124

Acclaim for Dianne Warren's The Wednesday Flower Man:

"Dianne Warren's women are often in a state of emotional disarray that sometimes borders on desperation, but they don't want sympathy. They come to grips with their problems on their own terms, sometimes successfully. They have inner reserves that see them through.

This is Warren's first book, and she reveals a strong and impressive ability to create credible characters.... The collection is relentlessly enjoyable, and Dianne Warren is a welcome addition to the long list of talented prairie writers."

William French, *The Globe and Mail*

"Warren does not contend with realistic imperatives alone. She entertains the surreal to make the real world bearable.... As does Margaret Atwood, Warren has a penchant for turning the existing world on its edge, making it appear just a trifle wacky, before she builds her fictions to contain not only what is apparent but what is slightly beneath reality."

Sharon Drache, *The Edmonton Journal*

"Dianne Warren is at her best in stories that deliberately distort the referential surface. In her successful stories, she begins with a verifiable context, with characters whose conflicts are familiar, who speak a language that is representational, and then moves into a world where logic no longer seems to apply and the dividing line between reality and fantasy becomes increasingly unclear. The stories suggest that one needs to go beyond realism to explore complex layers of reality.

C. Kanaganayakam, *Canadian Literature*

"The stories in Dianne Warren's *The Wednesday Flower Man* are feminist in the most basic (and most advanced) sense: the diversity of female experience is greater than the range of differences between men and women." D. French, *Books in Canada*

"The fifteen stories in *The Wednesday Flower Man* ... display an impressive range of imagination and technique.

The protangonists in most of these stories are women. The

two exceptions – 'Come Daylight,' in which a dying headstrong farmer subbornly refuses to reconcile with his estranged daughter, and 'Weak Hearts,' in which a resentful husband spitefully rejects his free-spirited wife – use men as ways of telling women's stories.

Warren's women are a desperate, interesting bunch, gritty with reality, even in the stories that go beyond it. They range from elderly middle-class women, like the widow futilely in love with the married doctor next door of 'Fine Bone China'; to working-class young marrieds, like the wife of the dispirited jobless man who turns to a revival meeting for marital salvation in the hilarious 'Miracles Nightly'; to watchful little girls like the one in 'The Elite Café' whose weary waitress mother has taken off for the next restaurant in the next town.

But in the most intriguing pieces, Warren goes beyond the limits of both the conventional short story and gender politics."

Dave Margoshes, *The Sunday Herald* (Calgary)

"Dianne Warren's *The Wednesday Flower Man* is a delightful collection of fifteen short stories. Warren ... has a gut feeling for human relationships.... Through it all, Warren weaves a thread of reality, nostalgia amd a great insight into human beings, and the result is a witty, semi-sweet collection of stories." *Star-Phoenix*

BAD LUCK
DOG

Dianne Warren

Aarian & Anne,
All the best.
Dianne Warren
Feb. 8/94

COTEAU BOOKS

Edited by Bonnie Burnard.
Cover painting "Big Dipper, Garbage Truck and Dog," oil on canvas board, 1990, by Richard Gorenko. Courtesy of Susan Whitney Gallery, Regina.
Painting photographed by Don Hall.
Author photograph by Don Hall.
Cover design by Kate Kokotailo.
Book design by Val Jakubowski and Shelley Sopher.
Typeset by Val Jakubowski.
Printed and bound in Canada.

Two of the stories in this collection have been previously published: "Big Otis and Little Otis" in *Canadian Fiction Magazine* and in *Lodestone: Stories by Regina Writers* (Fifth House, 1993) and "Safe House" in *Grain*.

The author wishes to thank Bonnie Burnard for her diligence in editing and her commitment to the manuscript; Connie Gault and Marlis Wesseler for their critical advice on earlier drafts of many of the stories; the Bombay Bicycle Club, still alive in spirit; and Coteau Books. She also wishes to acknowledge the financial support of the Saskatchewan Arts Board during the writing of some of these stories.

The publisher gratefully acknowledges the financial assistance of the Saskatchewan Arts Board, the Canada Council, and the City of Regina.

Canadian Cataloguing in Publication Data

Warren, Dianne, 1950 -

    Bad luck dog

    ISBN 1-55050-047-3

I. Title.

PS8595.A778B34 1993 C813'.54 C93-098027-1
PR9199.3.W377B34 1993

COTEAU BOOKS
401 - 2206 Dewdney Avenue
Regina, Saskatchewan
Canada S4R 1H3

Contents

Night Music

"If you had a retarded baby would you put it in an institution?"

The question came from the pregnant girl sitting beside Dell on the bus. The girl was in the window seat. It was getting dark outside, but even so Dell could see she wasn't more than fifteen or sixteen years old. Dell immediately wondered if the girl had been told by her doctor that there was something wrong with her baby, every pregnant woman's nightmare, but then she remembered the retarded boy who had boarded the bus a few towns back, and she concluded he had started the girl worrying. The boy had got on with his mother, talking a mile a minute, and for the life of her Dell had been unable to make out a word he'd been saying. His mother appeared to understand, either that or she did an award-winning job of pretending she did.

"An institution?" Dell asked the girl.

"Yeah. Like Valley View Centre in Moose Jaw. Some people drop their retarded kids off there and they never have to see them again if they don't want to."

"Really?" Dell said. She'd never heard of that. She'd heard of Valley View, of course, but thought it was a place for adults who weren't capable of working or looking after themselves. Dell looked at the girl. Did she know what she was talking about? "People just drop their children off there?" she asked. "That can't be true."

"It is," the girl said. "I've been there. I used to belong to this church group and we went on a tour once. Pretty funny really. We went on a bus like a bunch of tourists. We took lunches and afterwards we went to the wild animal park and had a picnic."

"You saw children?" Dell asked.

"You should see the kids that live there. Some of them are tied to their beds, to keep them from hurting themselves, a nurse told us. You should just see them. Great big kids, teenagers even, wearing diapers and tied to their beds. Unreal, eh? Anyway, I was just wondering. What I would do if it happened to me."

"It won't happen to you," Dell said. "Of course it won't."

"It could," the girl said. "I used to do a lot of dope and stuff. Before I knew I was pregnant. I quit as soon as I found out, but you never know. It might have been too late."

"I'm sure it wasn't," Dell said, trying to hide her shock. Dope, the girl had said. Freely, as though there was nothing wrong with it, as though it weren't illegal.

"Sometimes I think they lie to you, the doctors I mean," the girl said. "Sometimes I think they say everything's fine all the time, no matter what, because that's the easiest. And I can understand that. It must be a lot harder to say everything's not fine. Then you'd have to deal with crying and panicking and all that. And what's the point if you can't do anything about it?"

"My goodness," Dell said. "You're thinking much too seriously for someone your age. And I'm sure everything will be fine. Look at you, the picture of health."

"Yeah," the girl said. "I take care of myself now."

The girl looked out the bus window and Dell thought, what a funny child. She couldn't remember talking to anyone who had said so many serious things in such a short time. Anyone, and especially not a teenager.

Dell turned around to look at George, who was sitting in the seat behind her. They hadn't been able to sit together because the bus was too crowded. Dell had picked out the pregnant girl as someone who would be safe to sit with.

"That must be your husband back there, I guess," the girl said.

"Yes," said Dell. "He's asleep."

"I wish I could sleep," the girl said. "With this baby kicking me in the ribs all the time, I never get any sleep."

"He's getting you ready for when you have to get up every few hours to feed him," Dell said. "Just you wait."

"I won't mind," said the girl, looking out the window again.

"You must be grandparents by now," she said a few minutes later.

"How could you tell?" Dell asked, not sure whether to be pleased she looked kindly, or insulted that she looked old. She wasn't that old, really. She and George were young grandparents. Both of their daughters had married within a few years of graduating from highschool.

"Lucky guess," the girl said. "Lately I've been putting people into categories. My age, parents, grandparents. Like that. I guess I'm about to move into a new category."

"When are you due?" Dell asked.

"In about a month," the girl said. "The first one's usually late, though. So I've heard. But then again, someone told me teenagers tend to have early babies, so who's to say."

"You can never tell," Dell said. "If you get your mind set one way or the other, you're sure to be wrong. Best to leave it up to the baby and be prepared for anything."

"Good advice," said the girl. "I can see you're a practical kind of person. That's the kind of person I'm trying to be now." She reached into her bag and pulled out a radio with headphones.

"How far are you going?" she asked Dell.

"Regina," Dell said.

"Me too." The girl fiddled with the headphones, trying to get the wires untangled. "Is that where you live?" she asked.

"No," Dell said. "We live on a farm near the border. We're just going to the city for a visit."

"Me too," the girl said. "I'm going to stay with my sister until the baby's born. She says it's better to have your baby in a big city hospital. They have better equipment and all that. And they have these special delivery rooms that are like bedrooms. She says you have at least a chance to keep your dignity if you have a baby in one of those rooms."

Dell didn't know what to say to that. She had never thought it possible to keep your dignity while having a baby, and she had no idea why so many women these days wanted their husbands present. She couldn't imagine George being there when her two had been born.

"We don't like the city much," Dell said. "But George's brother passed away not long ago and we thought we should go and stay with his widow for a while. She's had it pretty rough."

"You must be nice people," the girl said.

"We try to be," Dell said.

The girl arranged the radio headphones over her ears. "Don't mind me," she said. "I don't mean to be rude or anything. I just like to listen to music in the dark. When it's dark the music kind of fills up the world."

"You go ahead," Dell said. "I'm feeling a bit sleepy. Maybe I'll try to catch a few winks."

The girl switched on her radio and Dell closed her eyes. She thought she could hear George snoring in the seat behind her. She opened her eyes again and leaned around to see. Sure enough, he had his head back and his mouth wide open, his Toronto Blue Jays cap askew on his head.

"George," she said. He sat up with a start.

"George, lean your head to the side. Use your coat for a pillow."

George looked at her as though he truly did not know what she was talking about.

"You were snoring, George. Lean your head to the side."

George leaned his head back and closed his eyes again without following her instructions.

"Just let me sleep, Dell," he said. "It might be the last peace I get until we're home again."

The bus depot in Regina was crowded. Dell stood with the bags while George walked through the crowd looking for Fay or one of the kids. She tried to keep her eye on the pregnant girl, as the city bus depot at night didn't seem like the best place for a girl alone.

"You can wait with me here, if you like," Dell had said to her when they got inside, but the girl had said she'd be fine on her own and had wandered off, eight months pregnant, with two big bags slung over her shoulders. She'd disappeared in the crowd.

Dell lost sight of George too, and she began to feel uncomfortable. She had been in this bus depot many times, and each time she grew anxious without being able to explain why. She had been warned about pickpockets and drug addicts, but she wasn't afraid. There were too many people around to be afraid. There was something else, something that hit her as soon as she walked through the double doors into the waiting room. She looked around and wondered if other people felt the same way.

George came back and said he couldn't see Fay anywhere.

"I guess I'd better phone," Dell said, digging in her purse for change and Fay's phone number. She left George with the bags and made her way to the pay phones. After half a dozen rings, a male voice answered. It was a teenager's voice.

"Frank?" Dell said.

"Ah, no," the voice said.

"Oh," said Dell. "Well, is Fay there? Frank's mother?"

"Just a minute."

Dell heard the phone clunk as though it had been dropped to the floor. A man approached her and she caught his eye, quite by accident. She quickly turned her back to him, clutching her purse. She tried to watch him out of the corner of her eye and she was relieved when he turned away. Fay came on the line.

"Hello."

"Fay? It's Dell."

"Dell?"

"Dell. George's wife." Dell felt impatience creeping into her voice and tried to control it. She's a widow, she told herself. A new widow.

"Oh. Dell. How nice of you to call."

"Fay, we're here," Dell said. "In Regina. Remember, I phoned to tell you we were coming. You said you'd meet us at the bus depot. Or send Frank or Jeannie. Do you remember?"

Dell heard the phone drop again.

"Frankie!" she heard Fay shout. "It's your Auntie Dell and Uncle George. They're at the bus."

"Fay!" Dell called into the phone. "Fay, never mind. We'll take a taxi."

"Frankie, do you hear me? Get downtown right away and pick them up."

"Fay, it's all right. Never mind. " Dell was shouting into the phone now and she became conscious of people looking at her. She grew embarrassed. Fay came back on the line.

"I can't make him do anything, " she said. "He won't do a thing for me."

"Never mind. He's probably busy with his friends. We'll take a taxi."

"Don't let them charge you too much," Fay said.

"I'm sure they won't," Dell said, and hung up.

On the way back to George, she saw the pregnant girl. She was leaning against a wall of orange lockers, her radio headphones still on, her bags at her feet.

"Is your sister coming to get you?" Dell asked her.

The girl nodded, taking off her headphones and hanging them around her neck.

"Listen," Dell said. "I'd really like to send you a little something for the baby. Would you mind giving me your sister's address?" She took out her address book and gave it to the girl. "I hope I'm not being too forward," Dell said. "It's just that I like picking out things for babies."

The girl wrote the address in Dell's book.

"That would be really nice," she said to Dell, handing the book back to her.

"You take care of yourself," Dell said.

She put the address book back in her purse and looked for George. She saw all the people waiting, leaning against walls and pillars, sleeping on benches, and she was desperate to get out. All the waiting was driving her mad. She found George and grabbed him by the arm.

"Quick," she said to him. "I think I saw a taxi pull up out front. We can get it if we hurry."

George picked up the bags and followed her out to the street. There were four or five taxis waiting. They had their pick.

There was a party going on at Fay's. George and Dell could hear it as soon as the taxi pulled up in front of the house. George paid the taxi driver and he pulled away, leaving them standing on the sidewalk.

"Godalmighty," George said.

"It's a wonder the neighbours don't complain," Dell said. "I suppose in the city you just get used to this."

"I might as well tell you right now," George said, picking up the bags, "that I am not going to be able to stop myself from saying this was a stupid idea."

"Don't say it yet," Dell said. "We're not even in the door."

Dell started up the walk. There were no drapes in the front

window and she could see Frank and four or five other teenagers through the glass. She thought, who would go without drapes in their front window, especially in the city? She was about to start up the front steps when she thought she saw flames in the living room.

"Jesus H. Christ," George said. "The house is on fire." He dropped the bags, bolted past Dell and threw open the door. Dell followed.

The front door opened directly onto the living room. In the middle of the floor was an old tripod barbecue with some sticks burning in it. Several pieces of firewood lay on the floor and Frank was getting set to put one on top of the kindling. The house was filling up with smoke.

"Just what in hell do you think you're doing?" George bellowed.

The teenagers looked at him. They all had cans of beer in their hands.

"Uncle George," Frank said.

"Hey. It's Farmer Dan," one of the other boys said.

"Where's your mother?" George asked Frank.

"In the kitchen," Frank said.

"Fay?" Dell called.

"She's listening to the police radio," Frank said.

"Put that fire out, boy," George said. Dell could only think how glad she was that George had come with her instead of staying home as he had threatened to do.

"She said we could," Frank whined. He sounded like a small boy, only his voice was deep.

"I think the party's over, Frankie," a boy sitting on the couch said. He had sunglasses on. A girl sat on his knee, the only girl there. She was wearing a black strapless top and skin-tight black jeans with silver studs down the outside seams. She smiled ambiguously, like she didn't know if what was happening was good or bad. The boy pushed her off his knee and stood up. "Come on, Frankie. Let's go."

"Mom!" Frank called.

Fay appeared in the doorway. She screamed when she saw the fire, ran back to the kitchen, then appeared again with a plastic jug of water, which she threw on the barbecue. The barbecue had rust holes in the bottom and black water dripped onto the carpet.

"What the hell's going on here?" she asked.

"You said we could," Frank whined.

"I said you could barbecue burgers in the back yard, for Christ's sake."

"You liar," Frank said.

"Watch it, boy," George said. "You watch how you talk to your mother."

Dell cringed. They'd been here only minutes and already things were out of hand.

"Never mind," Fay said. "He's good for nothing. You hear me, Frankie? Good for nothing."

The teenagers were all moving toward the doorway. They moved slowly, finishing beers and eyeing George defiantly. The girl was still smiling. She had no jacket, and when she followed the boys outside her bare shoulders brazenly caught the streetlight.

Frank grabbed his jean jacket from where it was lying on the floor and picked up the huge cassette player that was still blasting loud music. He moved to the door with the cassette player on his shoulder, then turned to Fay and said, "You're a fucking cow." He was out the door before George could reach him. George started to follow, but Dell jumped in front of him.

"Let him go, George," she said.

The music moved down the walk and into a car that was parked on the street.

"I hope the hell he never comes back," Fay said. "I hope the police catch him for something and throw him in jail."

"He'd better not come back," George said. "Not as long as I'm here."

"Oh dear," Dell said. Her eyes were stinging from the smoke, and she was thinking that the smell would linger in the furniture, find its way into the walls, the baseboards. It was a smell you could never get rid of. She looked at the black mess on the carpet and said, "Maybe we'd better carry the barbecue outside."

George knew what that meant, the *we* part. He carried it out and set it on the front lawn. Dell went around the house opening windows, then she got a rag from the kitchen and tried to clean the sooty water out of the carpet. George came back in carrying their bags, which Frank had apparently given a few good kicks on his way past. Fay seemed to have gone into some kind of trance. She

stood in the doorway between the living room and the kitchen as
Dell cleaned and George took the firewood outside. Chips of bark
with some kind of little black bugs crawling on them were left on
the carpet. Dell could hear the police radio crackling in the
kitchen. Every once in a while a dispatcher's voice would come on
giving code numbers and addresses, and Fay would say, "There's
been a fender bender at Albert and Twenty-fifth. Miles away." Or,
"That one's an armed robbery. The 7-Eleven on Fourth. Walking
distance from here."

Dell got the soot cleaned up as best she could and asked Fay
where her vacuum cleaner was.

"Don't have one," Fay said dreamily from the doorway. "Not
one that works anyway."

Dell and George exchanged glances. Dell got the broom and
tried to sweep up the chips of bark, but the broom kept catching in
the carpet. She ended up picking the chips out of the carpet by
hand.

"Do you have any bug spray?" she asked Fay. "Raid, or
anything like that?"

The radio crackled and the dispatcher's voice came on. Fay
held her hand up, indicating she was busy listening.

"Domestic dispute," Fay said after the voice was silent. "In
those apartments over on McIntosh." She said it as though Dell
and George should know exactly what apartments she meant.
"They'll probably send out the MFC Unit," Fay said. "Mobile
Family Crisis. Or is it Family Mobile Crisis. Or Family Crisis
Mobile. Now I'm confused. I can't seem to think straight."

"Come and sit down," Dell said. "I've got this just about taken
care of." She picked up the empty beer bottles and took them past
Fay into the kitchen. On her way back she gently took Fay's arm
and led her to the couch.

"You've had it awfully rough, Fay," Dell said. "George and I
are here to help. We'll do whatever we can."

"I haven't seen Jeannie for over two weeks," Fay said. "And
now Frankie's gone too."

"Good riddance," said George, under his breath, but Dell heard
him.

"George," Dell said. "Would you take our bags to the bedroom. Which bedroom should we sleep in, Fay?"

"Jeannie's, I guess. There's not much chance she'll be back."

"Jeannie's room," Dell said to George, and he took the bags.

"Did I tell you Jeannie's singing now out at the racetrack?" Fay asked. "I saw an ad in the paper. Well, *I* didn't see it, but my neighbour did. She cut it out and gave it to Frankie to give to me. Wasn't that nice of her?"

"The racetrack? Why would she be singing at the racetrack?" Dell asked.

"They have a bar out there. Or a lounge I guess it's called." Fay jumped up and went to the table where the telephone was. "I kept the ad," she said, rummaging in a pile of papers. "I know I kept it. I wanted to show it to Frankie."

"You just said Frankie gave you the ad, Fay. Didn't you just say that?"

"Did I? I don't remember." She gave up looking. "I don't know about Frankie," she said. "He's still such a baby. He's sixteen and a half and he's still such a baby."

Dell looked at Fay standing alone in the middle of the room. She was thin as a rail and her wrists were the size of a little girl's. If Dell hadn't known Fay for almost twenty years she would think she were ill, dying of cancer maybe. But Fay had always looked like that.

"Perhaps Frankie's got in with a bad crowd," Dell suggested. "I didn't really like the look of those boys who were here."

"Jeannie quit school, you know," Fay said. "She was always pretty good at school, but she quit anyway."

"Oh dear," Dell said. "Well, I'm sorry to hear that. She would have graduated this year, wouldn't she?"

"I don't know what's wrong with kids these days," Fay said.

"The world's a frightening place for them," Dell said. "I think that has something to do with it."

"I don't know where Jeannie's living," Fay said.

Dell didn't know what to say to that. "Do you think we should call the police?" she asked. It sounded lame before the words were even out.

"She's eighteen now," Fay said. "You can't call the police when they're eighteen."

"Not even if you're worried about them? Surely if you're worried something's happened— "

"I guess she thinks that boyfriend is going to look after her," Fay interrupted. She looked at Dell. "You remember him, don't you?"

Dell shook her head. She tried to remember if Jeannie had been with anyone at Earl's funeral, but she didn't think she had. Quite the opposite, in fact. Jeannie had given the very strong impression at the funeral that she was alone. She'd even sung a solo during the service, without accompaniment. Dell and George had squirmed at the inappropriateness of the song, "Love Me Tender," but when Jeannie was finished she tossed her hair back and said, "It was his favourite," so how could they criticize?

"Does she earn money as a singer?" Dell asked.

"Oh, he's good-looking all right," Fay said, "but that's not everything."

George called to Dell from the bedroom and she went to see what he wanted.

"Jesus Christ, Dell," George said, "I wouldn't get into this bed if it was the last bed on earth and I hadn't slept for a year." He was staring at the filthy sheets on Jeannie's bed.

"Fay," Dell called, "where do you keep your clean sheets? Don't trouble yourself. Just tell me where, and I'll get them."

"She won't have any clean sheets," George said. "God-almighty, this is a nightmare."

Fay didn't answer. Dell went looking in the closets and when she didn't find any clean sheets she took the dirty ones downstairs and put them in the washing machine. There was an opened box of detergent on the floor, but by the layer of dust on the white powder Dell could see it hadn't been used for a while. After she put the sheets and some towels in the machine, she went back upstairs and told George to go for a walk around the block or something until the bed was ready. He did. Dell joined Fay at the kitchen table, where she was listening to the police radio. There was a water glass of something amber-coloured on the table in front of her. Dell could guess what it was.

"Another armed robbery," Fay told Dell. "And a pile-up on the Ring Road. There's a fire too, at the CANCO oil upgrader. They have fires out there all the time. If I had a car I might go and see it. I do that sometimes. But Frankie's got the car. I guess it's his now. Where he gets the money for gas, I don't know."

"Perhaps his friends chip in," Dell said.

"Why do they have so many fires at the upgrader?" Fay asked. "They can't seem to put them out. I wonder if it's the same fire over and over again, or a different one each time."

Dell thought again that Fay looked exhausted, but of course that wasn't surprising. Her husband had been dead a month, Jeannie was gone, and Frank was turning out exactly the way everyone expected him to. Not that Earl had been much different, but Dell would never complain about Earl out loud. George could if he wanted to and had many times, but Dell felt it was his right because Earl had been his brother.

For a few brief moments after they'd got word that Earl was gone, Dell had wondered if maybe Fay's life would get better. But then she remembered what Fay was like and what Frank was like and she knew the solution wasn't as simple as Earl's death.

"Fay," Dell said. "You should go to bed."

"Oh no," Fay said. "Not yet. The night's just starting." She looked at the radio.

Dell sat at the table with Fay until the sheets were dry and George was back from his walk. Then she and George went to bed. All night they heard the radio crackling, the dispatcher's voice giving codes and instructions that meant nothing to them but gave the impression that what went on in the city at night was beyond anyone's control.

There was no food in the house. Dell wondered what Fay lived on, what she fed the kids. She peeked into Fay's bedroom and saw that she was asleep on top of the bed with her clothes still on from the night before. George wanted to go straight to the bus depot, but Dell said they couldn't just leave when they hadn't yet done a thing for Fay.

"There's no Christly food here, Dell," George said. "You can't even make coffee. I've got neighbours going out of their way to look after my livestock, and what for? There is nothing we can do."

"We could get her a few groceries," Dell said.

"How?" George wanted to know. "We've got no car. And damned if I'm paying for a taxi on top of her groceries."

Dell remembered from an earlier visit, from a time when Earl was still alive and Jeannie was taking singing lessons from a woman down the street, that there was a corner store a few blocks away. She'd walked there with Jeannie once, to get a quart of milk. Dell had bought the milk and Jeannie had bought a pack of cigarettes.

"Does your mother know you smoke?" Dell had asked on the way home.

"Of course she does," Jeannie had said. "She bums cigarettes from me. And don't give me any lectures about lung cancer. I've seen all those pictures of diseased lungs and they don't scare me a bit. My singing teacher is always telling me I shouldn't smoke, but I know lots of singers who do."

Dell told George about the store and they walked there together. They bought as many groceries as they could carry, even though the store was small and the food was overpriced. They didn't know where else to go. Dell made breakfast and called Fay from her bedroom doorway. Fay lifted her head and told her to go straight to hell.

"Go straight to hell," she said, looking right at Dell. "So you've got diamond earrings. So you have diamonds in your ears. Go to hell anyway."

Dell slowly shut the door.

"Did you hear that?" George asked.

"She wasn't talking to me," Dell said. Dell didn't own diamond earrings, so Fay couldn't have been talking to her. But to whom? Not Jeannie, surely not. And why hadn't Fay recognized her?

"I don't know what you're planning to do for her," George said, "but I wish you'd hurry up because I want to get the hell out of here."

"These things take time," Dell said.

"What things?" George asked, and Dell couldn't answer.

"Earl was your brother," she said. "Fay is your brother's wife."

"She's no relative of mine."

Dell felt herself getting angry.

George saw it. "And don't tell me I'm a mean son-of-a-bitch either," he said. "I'm not. I just recognize a hopeless case when I see it."

"She needs help."

"You just try helping her with those kids. You just try calling a spade a spade and see what happens."

"Maybe you should go home right now," Dell said, near tears. "Catch the next bus."

"I'm not leaving you here alone," George said.

"Why not?" Dell asked.

"Because I don't trust that Frank as far as I could throw him. I'm telling you, Dell. Wash the clothes. Clean up the house. But you heard what she said. You might not have diamonds in your ears, but that was you she was talking to."

"I don't think so," Dell said.

"I'm not saying another thing about it," George said. "Just do what you have to and do it fast."

Dell looked at Fay's empty glass on the table where she'd been sitting the night before, next to the black radio, now silent.

"I'll clean the house today," she said. "Maybe I can get Fay to help. It would do her good to get at something, even if it is only cleaning."

Fay slept all day. Dell cleaned and George went for walk after walk around the block. When he wasn't walking he was sitting on the front step staring at the neighbours and watching the cars go by.

"You could make yourself useful," Dell said once, but she couldn't think of anything for him to do.

Around five o'clock Fay got up. She walked into the kitchen where Dell was looking at an open drawer full of loose buttons, all colours and sizes. She'd found them while she was cleaning. They were only buttons, but in Fay's house Dell felt as though she'd opened a treasure chest.

"I dreamed that Elizabeth Taylor died," Fay said. "At least I think I dreamed it. Have you been listening to the radio? Maybe it's true."

At first Dell thought Fay meant the police radio. She almost laughed and said, "Really Fay. Do you think if Elizabeth Taylor died there would be an announcement on every police radio in North America?" Then she realized Fay meant the AM radio, and she said, "I don't think it's true. She almost died a while ago, from some respiratory thing, but she got over that. She's fine now, doing all that volunteer work for Aids."

"If I dreamed it, it's not good news either," Fay said, "because sometimes my dreams come true. They're premonitions."

Dell was still looking down into the drawer full of buttons. "My goodness," she said. "Where in the world did you get these? I've never seen so many buttons."

"Woolco," Fay said. "They sell them for two dollars a bag. If you buy them by the card, they're an arm and a leg." She walked over and picked up a handful, then let them drop through her fingers, back into the drawer. "They're so pretty," she said.

Dell was surprised to hear Fay say the word *pretty*. She would never have suspected it could come so easily from Fay's lips.

"I didn't know you sewed," Dell said.

"I used to," Fay said. "but not for a long time. I still buy buttons for some reason. Don't ask me why."

Fay got a bottle from the cupboard above the kitchen sink and poured herself a glass full of whatever was in it. She didn't offer Dell any. She switched on the police radio and sat down at the table.

"Do you mind that I made supper?" Dell asked.

"I don't mind," Fay said. She sniffed the air.

"It's beef stew," Dell said.

"Not that," Fay said. "It smells like smoke in here. Wood smoke."

"From the barbecue," Dell said. "Don't you remember?"

"We barbecued last night?" Fay asked. "I remember Frankie had some friends over. I remember I told him I wasn't going to cook for all his friends. Where is Frankie anyway? I'm surprised he isn't here. He'd want to see you."

"Frankie didn't come home last night," Dell said. "He left just when we got here and he hasn't been home since."

"Oh Christ," Fay said, looking suddenly frightened. "I hope nothing's happened to him. Nothing's happened to him, has it?"

Dell tried to sound reassuring. "I'm sure it hasn't. He'll be home tonight, I imagine."

"Little bugger," Fay said, pouring herself another drink. "Well, at least he got to see you for a few minutes then."

Around eleven Fay had a call from the police saying Frank was at the hospital. Dell and George were in bed, but they got up when they heard Fay on the phone. They could tell something was wrong.

Frank was all right, the police said. He'd been in a car accident though, and had some cuts on his face. He'd managed to drive Fay's car into a light standard and it was probably totalled.

"What time was the accident?" Fay wanted to know.

The policeman told her about nine-thirty.

"Nine-thirty," Fay said after she hung up. "Do you remember an accident on the radio at nine-thirty?" she asked Dell and George.

They didn't.

"How about that," Fay said. "My own kid's in an accident and I miss it on the radio." She looked distressed, like she might cry.

"Come on, Fay," Dell said quickly. "We'll call a taxi and go and pick him up."

"No," Fay said. "I'm not going."

"You're just going to leave him there?" Dell asked.

"I'm not going," Fay said. "Something might come over the radio. Something big."

"Oh, for Christ's sake," George said. "Which hospital is he at? Did you even remember to ask?"

"No," Fay said. "Wait a minute. I think they take all the car accidents to the Plains. That's where he'll be. The Plains."

"Call a taxi, Dell," George said. "We're about to do something useful."

In the taxi, Dell told George to keep control of his temper. "Don't go acting like a man and flying off the handle without thinking," she said.

"I've been doing a lot of thinking, Dell," George said. "I know what that kid needs."

"He's just a boy," Dell said. "Think of his home life. Think of the kindness he's missed out on."

"I've thought about all of that," George said. "And it doesn't change things."

"If you embarrass me," Dell said. "If you do something drastic ..."

They were quiet, and then Dell said, "Do you think we ought to take him back to the farm for a while?"

George looked at her. Dell could hear him asking her if she'd gone completely off her rocker, but he didn't. He surprised her by saying nothing.

"We don't have to decide right now," Dell said carefully. "But it's something to consider."

George tipped his cap back on his head and held one hand over his eyes, rubbing one temple with his thumb. Then he put his other hand over that one, as though one weren't enough.

"I hope you won't just write the idea off," Dell said.

"He'd never come," George said.

"He might," Dell said. "We won't know if we don't ask."

"Think about Fay," George said. "You think she's bad off now. Frank probably keeps her alive."

"That's not what children are for," Dell said.

George took his hands away from his eyes and looked at Dell, who was sitting close to the door on her side of the seat.

"Come here," he said.

"What?" Dell asked.

"Just come here. Slide over here."

She did, and George put his arms around her.

"What about Frank?" she asked.

"Shhhhh," George whispered.

"We have lots of room."

"Shhhhh."

He held her tightly. Dell was conscious of the taxi driver. He was a young man. She thought he would be laughing at them.

"The taxi driver," she said quietly.

"This is the city," George said. "He's just hoping we won't throw up all over the back seat of his car."

Dell laughed then, for the first time since they'd arrived at Fay's.

When they got to the hospital they were told by a nurse that Frank didn't seem to be there anymore.

"What do you mean, 'Doesn't seem to be here'?" George asked. His voice was loud.

"George," Dell said. "Control your temper."

The nurse looked at them. "I mean he isn't here," she said. "He doesn't seem to be. He seems to have left."

"Godalmighty," George said. "Isn't anybody in charge around here?"

"I can call the doctor," the nurse said. "If you'd like to talk to him."

"Just tell us," Dell broke in. "Did he seem to be okay? Will he be all right?"

"We patched him up," the nurse said. "He should have waited for you. We like to keep an eye on them, for concussion, you know. But what could we do? They were running all over the place. They'd been drinking, but the police couldn't charge anyone because they couldn't figure out who was driving."

Dell sighed. "I guess there's nothing to do but go home."

"A lot of money wasted on taxis tonight," George said. "And I don't imagine Fay will think to ask if she can pay us back."

"She has very little money, George."

"Enough to keep herself in booze," George said.

When they got back, Fay was sitting in front of the police radio with the ad for Jeannie's singing engagement in her hand.

"He's all right," Dell said to her. "They released him from the hospital. He's gone off with his friends. No-one's in any trouble." She hoped Fay wouldn't remember that her car was totalled. They could worry about that later.

"Look at the dates," Fay said to Dell, referring to the newspaper ad. "She's still there. She's still singing out at the racetrack. Ten until two every night except Sunday."

Dell sat down. "Fay," she said. "Would you like to go? Would you like to go and hear Jeannie sing?"

George shook his head, warning her.

"Go to bed, George," Dell said. "This will be girls' night out."

"It's after midnight, Dell," George said. "It's almost one o'clock."

"What do you say, Fay?" Dell asked. "I don't imagine people get dressed up much to go to the racetrack. We can probably go just as we are."

George left the room, throwing his wallet on the table in front of Dell as he passed.

Fay studied the newspaper ad. "She takes good pictures," she said. "Her picture would attract people, wouldn't it. Even if they didn't care for her singing, they might go just to look at her."

"Do you want to go?" Dell asked again.

Fay shook her head.

"I want to help you, Fay," Dell said. "I want to help you put your life together. We all have to pick up the pieces after a tragedy, after a death. We all have to go on."

"A death?" Fay asked. "There hasn't been a death, has there? You said Frankie was all right."

"Earl," Dell said, exasperated. "I meant Earl."

"Oh," Fay said. "Earl. Yes." She stared at Jeannie's picture in the ad. "There's another fire at the upgrader," she said after a bit. "I wouldn't mind going out there. We couldn't get very close, but once you get out on the prairie you can see a fire from miles away."

Dell called a taxi.

"You'll have to tell him where we want to go," she said to Fay as they got in the back seat. "I haven't a clue."

Fay gave the driver instructions. Dell thought he would think they were completely mad, dangerous possibly, but if he did, he didn't let on. He drove them out of the city, then turned off the freeway and headed toward a huge industrial complex.

"Is this okay?" he asked, parking on the shoulder of the gravel road. "You'll get a pretty good view from here." There was a big chain link fence around the upgrader property. Dell could see they wouldn't get any closer.

"This is fine," Fay said.

"We won't be long," Dell said to the driver. "We ... *she* just wanted to get a look at the fire."

Dell and Fay looked at the flame licking into the black sky. They couldn't tell what exactly was burning. It wasn't much of a fire. In fact, if Fay hadn't told her otherwise, Dell would have thought it was just a regular industrial fire, one that was supposed to be there, although there was something ominous about the black cloud that was building above the flame. Even against the dark sky, you could see it.

"I think it's the same fire," Fay said. "They keep trying to put it out, but it just keeps popping back up again. It doesn't always get into the paper, but I hear it on the police radio."

Dell listened for sirens and looked for flashing lights, but she couldn't see or hear anything.

"You know," Fay said in her dreamy voice, "it's a funny thing. I dream about Jeannie sometimes. She's singing and wearing a black dress with buttons all over it, buttons from my drawer in the kitchen. Isn't that odd."

"We can go and see her tomorrow night, if you like," Dell said.

"No," Fay said. "I don't believe I will."

"I think, then, that George and I will go home tomorrow," Dell said. "He's worrying about the livestock."

"I wish Frankie were here," Fay said. "This is the sort of thing Frankie would like. Fire. He's always liked fire. From the time he was a little boy. Do you remember when he lit the garage on fire?"

"No," Dell said. "I didn't hear about that."

"He poured gas for the lawnmower around and threw a match in it. He could have killed himself. I was terrified afterwards, when I thought about it."

"Well," Dell said. "Kids do things like that. Especially boys."

"Earl used to mow the lawn once in a while," Fay said. "I don't suppose anyone's mowed it since he died."

"Do you miss Earl?" Dell asked.

"Earl?" Fay said. "No. Not really. He used to hate it when I listened to the radio all night."

Dell thought, I will not be like George. I will not say she's hopeless. She isn't hopeless. She has no perspective, no way to put things in order and judge their value, but she is not hopeless.

"Not long after Earl died," Fay said, "this social worker came along. I don't know why. Because of Frankie I suppose. He's always in some kind of trouble. She was talking to me, but I couldn't hear her. It was the funniest thing. I could see her mouth working like crazy but I couldn't hear her, and I decided it was because everything she was saying was lies. It was all lies. I might even have told her that, I don't know for sure. And then I thought, these lies, these are what you have to tell me because you can't say the other, the truth, I mean. You can't be a social worker or a teacher or a politician and go around telling the truth. There would be no point. It just wouldn't make sense. Do you know what I mean?"

"Honestly, Fay," Dell said. "I have to say I do not know what you mean."

"It's quite simple really. The truth is frightening. You know that."

"What is the truth?" Dell asked. "The truth that is so frightening."

"The truth is, we are nothing. They aren't going to come around and tell me that, are they? 'You are nothing.' They aren't going to say that."

Dell picked up one of Fay's small hands. She expected her to pull away, but she didn't. "What is wrong with you, Fay?" Dell asked. "You aren't nothing. You shouldn't say that."

"Nothing," Fay said. "Zero."

"Can't you see that it's wrong to look at your life that way?" Dell said. "You can have a better life. You can get Frankie straightened out. You can have Jeannie back."

"I can't hear you," Fay said.

"You could quit drinking," Dell said.

"I can't hear you," Fay said. "You can talk all you want, but I can't hear you."

Dell dropped Fay's hand. She thought about the pregnant girl on the bus, the one she was going to buy the baby present for. "I met someone the other day," she said. "A girl in trouble, if you know what I mean. She didn't have much, you could tell, but she was trying to make her life better. She'd quit drugs and smoking, she told me, because of the baby."

"Lies," Fay said dreamily.

"No," Dell said. "She was telling the truth."

"The world's a frightening place," Fay said. "I heard you say that the other night."

"Frightening, yes," Dell said. "But not hopeless."

They looked at the fire. They watched the black smoke build in the sky above the flame and drift toward the city.

"I think your dream about Jeannie, the one with the buttons, means you want Jeannie to have a good life," Dell said.

"Look at that fire," Fay said. "It's like a monument, don't you think? It's like a fire burning over a big graveyard. I wish I could get right up to it. I wish I could get so close I could feel the heat burning my skin. I'd like to feel the smoke inside my lungs. I'd like to feel my lungs explode."

Dell felt herself shiver. It's the cold, she told herself, the cool night air. She knew, though, that it was Fay.

The taxi driver turned around and looked at them. "You've

seen enough, eh," he said. It wasn't a question. He started the car.

On the way back to town Fay got right up on the seat, on her knees, and faced backward so she could watch the fire out the rear window. Dell could hear her breathing deeply, sucking in air that was tinged with smoke. Dell thought, this is the most alive I have ever seen her. She was tempted to get up on the seat with Fay and try to figure out what the attraction was. Instead, she thought about how she and George would be leaving in the morning, about how they would go to the bus depot and be stranded only briefly among the people waiting.

"I'll get George to mow your lawn before we go," Dell said. "He'd be glad to do that for you."

"If he wants," Fay said. "It doesn't matter to me."

The fire was very small in the distance now, and Fay turned around and sat down on the seat. The driver turned on the radio. Music filled the darkness.

"Would you turn that off, please?" Fay asked the driver.

He did. Dell became aware of the meter ticking away. She wondered why she hadn't noticed it before and hoped she had taken enough money from George's wallet to pay the fare. She remembered what the pregnant girl said about listening to music at night and she thought, that girl is right, I know that girl is right.

As they reached the city limits, Fay lay down on the seat, her head almost on Dell's lap. She mumbled something. Dell thought it was, "Love me tender," but then she thought Fay couldn't have said that. It was too ridiculous. Just to be sure she asked, "What was that, Fay? What did you say?"

"Nothing much," Fay said. "Only I don't think they're ever going to get that fire out. I think they might as well let it burn."

That was all either of them said. Dell tried to sneak a look at the fire one last time but it was gone, swallowed by the city lights. She leaned against the door on her side and watched Fay, curled up, asleep, looking very much like a child who had resigned herself to a long journey.

The Curve of the Earth

THEY HAD the old woman carried down to the beach by Mr. Boone, the proprietor's handyman. Mr. Boone was a big man who had retired early from his job as a foreman in a warehouse. He had been a boxer at one time, a provincial heavyweight champion, so people said. Now he spent his summers at the lake doing maintenance on the cabins, and whatever else the proprietor asked him to do.

The proprietor had asked Mr. Boone to help Lydia get her mother down to the beach because he believed that if you treated your customers well they'd come back. In fact, Lydia and her family had been coming back to the same rented cabin every summer for as long as anyone could remember. The family had changed over the years, growing as young people got married and had children, then dwindling because of moves, deaths and divorces. This summer the family was down to Lydia, her niece Dora, Dora's son Lenny and Lydia's mother. Even Lydia's mother had tried to get out of coming. She told Lydia she was finally ready to admit out loud that she didn't like beaches and never had, and at eighty-six and a half years old she should be able to stay home if she wanted to. But Lydia convinced her that summer at the beach was a tradition, and what was a tradition without the matriarch?

Lydia's mother complained all the way from the cabin to the beach.

"I *can* walk, you know," she said, not to Mr. Boone, but to Lydia, who followed behind carrying two canvas lawn chairs and a yellow shade umbrella.

"I know you can walk, Mother," Lydia said, "but I'm trying to conserve your energy."

"I'd prefer to conserve my dignity," her mother said. "Besides, I'm going to sit in a chair on the beach. I don't need my energy for that."

"You're light as a feather, Mrs.," Mr. Boone said. "This is no trouble at all, absolutely no trouble."

"I've shrunk," Lydia's mother said. "I used to be a large woman. Do you remember that?"

"It is my policy," Mr. Boone said, "never to discuss with a woman any topic relating to her size."

"You were never very big, Mother," Lydia said. "You never wore larger than a size twelve."

"Ten years ago you wouldn't have been able to carry me," her mother said to Mr. Boone.

"Don't be so sure," Mr. Boone said. "I was ten years younger myself then."

"You don't have to worry about Mr. Boone, Mother," Lydia said. "He used to be a boxer."

Dora followed along behind Lydia, carrying a nylon gym bag that contained a picnic lunch and her grandmother's watercolours. Lenny walked with her, holding onto her arm. Dora told him when to pick up his feet so he wouldn't trip, and she urged him to hurry and keep up when she felt his weight on her arm.

"The boy does well, doesn't he?" Mr. Boone said, breathing heavily.

"Very well," said Lydia. "We're proud of him."

They were in the stand of trees that separated the lawns from the beach and Mr. Boone sidestepped along the path, trying to avoid any low-hanging spruce branches that might catch Lydia's mother in the face.

"You're not going to drop me, are you?" Lydia's mother asked.

"No, Mrs.," Mr. Boone said. Sweat was beginning to bead on his forehead.

"Because I'd be a lot worse off if you dropped me than I'd be if I fell on my own."

"Do you notice a difference in Lenny?" Lydia asked Mr. Boone. "From last summer, say?"

"Oh yes," said Mr. Boone. "A real difference."

"He's been learning to walk like a regular blind person, you know," Lydia said. "He takes your arm now, and trusts you to lead him along. When he was younger he would just sit down when he got outside. Just sit down on the ground and that would be that. Isn't that right, Dora?"

"Yes," Dora said. "He was afraid of the outside, because of all the sounds."

"The school has decided to treat him just like any other blind person," Lydia said. "He has other problems, you know, but they've decided there are certain skills he can learn, like walking outside. That's right, isn't it, Dora? Have I got that right?"

That's right, isn't it, Dora? Have I got that right? Lydia's mother thought Lydia sounded like a squawking gull. Everything she said sounded ordinary and pointless.

"Come on, hon," Dora said to Lenny. "We're almost there."

"He does very well indeed," said Mr. Boone, staggering a little.

"I do hope you're not going to drop me," Lydia's mother said.

"Stop fussing, Mother," said Lydia. "You'll drive Mr. Boone to distraction."

Lydia's mother could see the lake through the trees now. A horsefly was buzzing around her head, but she dared not swat at it in case she threw Mr. Boone off balance.

"Why aren't *you* going to this do tonight?" she asked Mr. Boone, trying to ignore the horsefly. "Lydia seems to think it will be the social event of the year."

"I'm not much for social events," Mr. Boone said. "To me, it's just another trip around the lake and I've been on plenty of those."

When they got to the private beach, which was just now deserted, Mr. Boone put Lydia's mother down, much to her relief. She held Mr. Boone's arm while she caught her balance.

"The lake's lovely today," she said.

The water was clear and calm, with just the odd ripple lapping the shore. A half-mile down was the crowded public beach and, just beyond it, the main pier. Music came up the beach from the sound system on the paddle wheeler, which was docked and waiting.

Lydia's mother could see that Mr. Boone was struggling to catch his breath. Lydia didn't seem to notice. She was busy setting up the lawn chairs.

"Are you all right?" Lydia's mother asked Mr. Boone.

"Oh yes," Mr. Boone said, using the sleeve of his T-shirt to wipe the sweat from his forehead. "A bit of a workout is good for a person."

"Don't fuss over Mr. Boone, Mother," Lydia said, digging the shade umbrella into the sand. "He's a sight younger than you are."

"I don't think we need that umbrella," her mother said. "The sun is going to set in a while. Look how low to the water it is."

The sun was, indeed, hovering in the west. Lydia ignored her mother's comment.

"Will that be all, then?" Mr. Boone asked, still trying to catch his breath.

"Thank you so much," Lydia said.

"Yes, thank you, Mr. Boone," her mother said, "although I want you to know that it was my daughter and not me who thought this carrying business up."

Mr. Boone went back through the trees and Dora seated Lenny in one of the canvas chairs. She placed the bag she'd been carrying next to the other chair, where her grandmother could easily get at it.

"I don't know if he's going to like this chair," Dora said. "Maybe I should have brought the lounger."

"He seems to be taking to it," said Lydia.

Lenny was bent over, feeling the legs and arms of the chair.

"I don't know, Aunt Lydia," Dora said. "Maybe we shouldn't go."

"Don't waste a minute worrying about us," her grandmother said. "Lenny and I know how to pass the time sitting in lawn chairs."

"Mother," Lydia said. "You needn't be so difficult. You have to agree that Dora is due for a bit of fun."

"Fun," her mother said. "Yes, I suppose one ought to have fun. Fun is not insignificant."

"We aren't nuns, you know," Lydia said.

"You'd be in big trouble with the Pope if you were," her mother said.

"What do you know about the Pope?" Lydia said, checking the lunch bag and setting it back down again. "Everything seems to be here," she said. "I guess we can go now, Dora."

Lydia's mother gazed out over the water. She knew Lydia was waiting for her to sit down, like a mother waiting for a child to settle in bed before she turned out the light. "Most of my life I didn't think about things," Lydia's mother said.

"Oh for Pete's sake," Lydia said.

"I was far too busy and entirely too healthy."

"Mother," Lydia said, "Dora and I really must get going."

"When you're my age you find yourself thinking. You can discover something in one day that turns everything in circles."

"Are you going to watch this child while we go out," Lydia said, "or do I have to go back for Mr. Boone?"

"You wouldn't ask Mr. Boone to baby-sit, surely," her mother said.

"To carry you back to the cabin," Lydia said. "If you don't want to watch Lenny, we might as well go back."

"Of course I'll watch Lenny," her mother said sharply. "I didn't say I wouldn't, did I. A few hours on the beach will be good for him. He's been in the cabin all day."

"Fine then," said Lydia.

"Fine," said her mother. She sat down and began taking off her shoes and socks.

"What are you doing?" Lydia asked.

"I'm going to put my toes in the water, if you have no objection."

"The water is very cold," Lydia said. "You won't like it."

"I think I can judge that for myself," her mother said.

"But Dora and I don't want to be late," said Lydia.

"Stop whining, Lydia," her mother said. "It's very irritating. And do I have to be seated when you leave, for heaven's sake?"

"Yes," Lydia said. "I don't want to be worrying that you fell over in the lake and drowned." Then she added, "It would be best for Lenny. He'll be fine as long as you're in the chair next to him. Isn't that right, Dora?"

"I suppose," Dora said.

"As long as you're talking, he'll know you're there and he'll think everything is normal," said Lydia. "Isn't that right, Dora?"

"I guess so," Dora said.

"I see," said her grandmother. "Well then, I'd better be quick."

"You're going to go in the water anyway, then?" Lydia said. "Even though Dora and I have to go?"

"Yes," said her mother. She tucked her thin white socks into her shoes and stood up in the sand.

"Really, Aunt Lydia," Dora said. "We're not in that much of a hurry."

"You are as stubborn as a mule," Lydia said to her mother.

"The sand feels warm on the bare feet," Lydia's mother said. "Do you think Lenny would like to have his shoes and socks off?"

"I don't think so," said Dora. "It might confuse him." Dora fished in the bag for a few plastic toys and placed them in Lenny's lap. "Here are your toys, hon," she said. "Don't throw them in the sand."

Lenny felt in his lap and picked up a plastic giraffe. He flipped it repeatedly against his cheek, making a soft, slapping sound.

"I think he'll be okay," Dora said. "You can tell when he's not happy because he throws his toys away."

Lydia's mother stepped down to the water and put her feet in. She found it was, as Lydia had said, very cold. Like ice, in fact. Still she stayed there for a few minutes, her ankles aching, watching Lenny play with the giraffe in the canvas chair. The sun was shining on him in spite of the umbrella.

She waded back out of the water and said, "It's not so bad. I don't know why you think it's cold, Lydia. I'm tempted to go in for a swim. Would anyone like to come with me?"

"Really, Mother," Lydia said. Then she said, "Another day maybe. Dora and I have to go."

"I guess he'll be all right," Dora said, looking at Lenny.

"Of course he'll be all right," her grandmother said. "I'm quite capable of taking care of the child. Anyway, I *am* being difficult, as Lydia says. You go ahead and don't worry." She stepped carefully toward the chairs, her wet feet gathering sand, and sat down.

"There," she said. "I'm seated. Everything is quite normal and you can leave now."

"Bye, hon," Dora said to Lenny. "I'm going out for just a bit. Great-grandma will look after you."

"The paddle wheeler will go right by here," Lydia said. "So

watch for us. We'll wave from the deck."

Lydia began walking in the direction of the public beach, then she turned and said, "By the way, mother. Your watercolours are in the bag with the picnic."

"My watercolours? Who said I wanted my watercolours?"

"I just thought you might do a sunset," Lydia said. "You haven't done a sunset in ages. Not that I've seen, anyway."

"Honestly Lydia," her mother said. "You are the limit."

Lydia began walking down the beach again and Dora followed her. They were both wearing turquoise blue sandals that Lydia had found on sale in a shop in town, and Lydia stopped to unbuckle hers so she could walk barefoot.

"I've gone off sunsets," Lydia's mother called out. Then she called, "I hope you run smack into Mr. Right. Two Mr. Rights, wearing matching shoes."

"Honestly mother, *you* are the limit," Lydia called back.

Lydia and Dora walked along the shore and Lydia's mother watched until they became indiscernible from the rest of the people at the public beach.

"I sometimes wonder why she is on this earth," Lenny's great-grandmother said to him after Lydia and Dora were out of earshot. "That's a terrible thing to say, and I would never say it to anyone but you, but there you are. Sometimes I wonder, and I can't help it."

"Can't help it," said Lenny.

"That's right. Well then. What shall we talk about? Music? Do you hear music from up the beach?"

"Hear music," Lenny said.

"Everything is different when it's just you and I, Lenny," she said.

Lydia's mother watched the paddle wheeler pull away from the pier and move toward them on a course parallel to the beach. It was decorated with patio lanterns, and as it got closer she could see perhaps twenty people on the upper deck. This was the last paddle wheeler tour of the summer and in recent years it had turned into a rather exclusive party, at least as exclusive as things got at the lake. Lydia had bought the tickets weeks earlier.

If the weather were inclement, the partygoers would be below

out of the wind or rain. Because it was such a nice evening, they
were all on the deck and Lydia's mother could watch their gala
affair, from a distance anyway, as long as the boat was visible from
the beach. She couldn't pick Lydia and Dora out though. She
wished she had binoculars with her so she could watch them and
try to decipher the meaning of what Lydia called fun.

"Here they come," she said to Lenny as the boat moved
directly in front of them. "Can you hear the music? Perhaps we
can sing along." She listened, but she didn't recognize the tune.

"I don't know what that music is," she said to Lenny. "It's
something modern, I suppose. You don't recognize it either, do
you. Neither of us does. I'm too old and you're ... well, you're just
the way you are."

"Way you are," said Lenny.

She watched the paddle wheeler as it passed, perhaps a quarter-
mile from shore, and she thought she saw someone wave from the
deck. The boat continued on its course along the beach, the sound
of music diminishing as it moved away, and then it disappeared
behind an island to the north.

"They're gone," the old woman said to Lenny. Then she said,
"Why would you care? You can't see them anyway."

"Can't see them," Lenny said.

"You know," his great-grandmother said, "our conversations
are very shallow. Have you noticed?"

Lenny didn't respond.

"On the other hand," she said, "I must say that I enjoy them as
much as any conversations I have with anyone. Isn't that
strange?"

"Strange," said Lenny. He began to rock gently in his chair,
saying, "Strange, strange, strange," over and over in rhythm with
his rocking. Each time he said the word *strange* he flipped the
plastic giraffe against his cheek. It all seemed very well organized.

"Lenny, Lenny, Lenny," his great-grandmother said. She had a
thought. "Would you like to take your shoes and socks off? The
sand feels quite wonderful."

She got up out of her chair and knelt, with difficulty, in front
of him. Lenny stopped rocking when he sensed her there, and she
undid his running shoes and slipped them off. Then she took off
his socks.

"Put your feet in the sand, Lenny," she said. "Try it."

Lenny dropped the plastic giraffe in his lap and slid forward in his chair so that his feet touched the sand. He pulled them back quickly, then he gingerly lowered them until they touched the sand again. This time, he left them there.

"Now I'm going to bury your feet," his great-grandmother said. "Cover them right up in this nice warm sand."

She made little piles over each of Lenny's feet and he didn't protest.

"See," she said. "I told you you'd like it."

The old woman struggled to her feet. Her back and knees were stiff, so she walked along the water's edge for a bit to stretch herself out before she sat down again in the chair next to Lenny.

She was about to say something to him about the noisy gulls overhead when she noticed that he had become absolutely still. He was sitting in the same position, his hands gripping the arms of the chair, his feet covered with sand, but he was motionless, hardly breathing, quite like a statue. She watched him with curiosity. What was he doing? Was he listening to some sound that she hadn't noticed? Perhaps he was fascinated by the gulls, or perhaps he was listening for the music from the paddle wheeler. Then she noticed grains of sand shifting ever so slightly on the little piles over his feet, and she realized he was focused on the sand, as though he had discovered a new mystery, one that could be solved only by intense concentration. She had to clear her throat and take a few deep breaths before she was able to speak. Even then, she hated to distract him.

"Do you like the sand, Lenny?" she finally asked when she saw him relax in his chair.

Lenny didn't say anything.

"In my old age," she said, "I can imagine the impact of suddenly knowing the earth is round and not flat. We are at a great disadvantage, Lenny, when we cannot feel the impact of the discoveries." She had an idea. "Would you like to feel the sand all over you? Lie in the sand, Lenny. Lie down. You'll like it."

Lenny slid off his chair and sat in the sand, his plastic toys spilling around him.

"Lie down," his great-grandmother said. "Go on. Lie down."

He did, and she began to cover him up with sand. He lay very still. She covered him entirely, except for his head. It was hard work but she kept at it even though her arms and legs ached and she felt a familiar pain in her chest. The pain was angina and she supposed it would be the end of her some day before too long.

When Lenny was a mound of sand with only his head visible, she stopped. She stood puffing, and then she realized the sun was shining full on Lenny's face. She decided that was not good for his eyes, even if he was already blind, so she struggled to pull the shade umbrella from where Lydia had planted it. She dug it into the sand again so that it protected Lenny's face from the sun.

"There," she said. "Now everything is perfect. Until you are tired of it, of course, and I'm sure you'll let me know when you are."

She sat in the chair again and watched Lenny's face, a picture of thought. She looked at the sky across the lake where a sunset was just beginning to intensify. She thought about her water-colours in the bag, and she reached down and lifted them onto her lap. She was tempted, but really, she had done enough sunsets in her day. In fact, the world had more sunset paintings by far than it needed. There was no discovering left to do, as far as sunsets went.

She looked at Lenny and imagined experiencing things the way he did. She closed her eyes and tried to feel what he felt lying under the sand. She felt the warmth of the sun. It was wonderful. She forgot about the indignities of being old, about the angina and the other aches and pains of an old body. Without opening her eyes, she pulled her dress up as far as was decent so she could feel the sun on her legs. She imagined the colours of a sunset spreading up her legs and through her body, brushing against her heart like so many pink and orange ribbons. She imagined the sound of colours, purple and blue hissing and humming inside her head, lulling her into a delicious dream state. She laughed, perhaps out loud, and she heard another laugh mix with hers. Lenny's. She imagined the revelation of discovering that the world was round, of being freed of the terrible belief that if you went one step too far you would fall off the edge. You could not fall off the edge. It was impossible. She imagined that she was free to travel the globe, around and around forever, knowing she could not fall off. The liberation was dizzying.

She woke up with a start. She could not see the boy. Her heart pounded with the realization that he was gone and the thought that he could have wandered into the water and drowned.

"This can't be," she said, struggling to her feet. Panic brought the pain back to her chest. She looked at the water, but saw nothing. She thought to look for footprints in the sand, but her eyes saw just one flat, beige plane with no contours or indentations, no features whatsoever. Then she realized her vision was blurred from sleep and she rubbed her eyes and blinked to try to clear them.

The spot where Lenny had risen from the pile of sand slowly came into focus. She saw the hollow where he had been, and she saw where the sand had dropped as he stood up, remembered him laughing as he felt the weight fall away. There were footprints leading from the hollow, away from the water and toward the line of trees. As she looked at the footprints, she was overtaken by relief.

And then she was overtaken by the spirit of Lenny's adventure. He had gone exploring. He was as brave and inquisitive as those men who had tested the edges of the earth with their boats. She followed Lenny's footprints toward the trees.

It was beginning to grow dark. She had no idea where she was in relation to the beach or the cabins. She knew that she could not have gone far though, as she had not stopped to put her shoes back on and she'd been forced to travel very slowly. The underbrush had cut into the bottoms of her feet. They'd stung at first, but now they were numb.

"Lenny," she called out, for perhaps the hundredth time. She stopped and listened. She could hear nothing but the frantic chatter of a squirrel overhead.

She tried to think which way Lenny would have gone, and what would have determined the direction he chose. She closed her eyes and felt the space in front of her with her hands, as Lenny might have done. Nothing. There were no clues. She continued walking in the direction that looked freest of deadfall, picking her way through the underbrush and the tree roots. Eventually she crossed a narrow trail through the bush and, because it seemed to offer easier walking, she followed it.

She knew that Lydia and Dora would be back from their party, and she imagined them finding the empty chairs and wondering what had happened. It occurred to her that Lydia was going to be very angry. Even if Lenny had been found and there was no reason to worry about him, Lydia would be furious. It would be useless to try to explain. What Lydia would see was an old woman who had fallen asleep at the beach, and then gone into the bush on her own to look for Lenny when she should have called immediately for help. She would see her mother's cut and bleeding feet as proof positive of her foolishness.

She walked until it became too dark to see, and she called Lenny until she had no voice left. The bottoms of her feet hurt again and she was tired, so very tired that every step took incredible effort. When she came to a tree that had fallen and blocked the path, she sat down on it. The spirit of adventure was gone, and she knew that Lenny was frightened and alone somewhere in this dark forest. She had to find him, but she could not go on.

Mr. Boone found Lydia's mother. It was dark and he came along the path with a flashlight. When the old woman saw it, she couldn't tell what it was, knew only that a strange light was bobbing up and down and sweeping the bush on both sides of the path. Her first instinct was to hide, to slip down behind the fallen tree and crouch like a rabbit, waiting for the danger to go away, but the urge to hide left her almost as soon as it came, and she called out instead.

"Hello," she called, as though she were greeting a visitor coming up her front walk. The light stopped, then swept the path and found her. She covered her eyes.

"Mrs.?" said Mr. Boone. "Is that you?"

She recognized his voice. "Yes, Mr. Boone, it is I. Have you found the boy?"

"Lenny?" Mr. Boone said, coming toward her.

"Yes," she said. "Have you found him?"

"Lenny's back at the cabin," Mr. Boone said.

"Thank God," she said. "He wandered into the bush, you know."

"Into the bush?" Mr. Boone said. He sounded puzzled.

"Yes," she said. "That's what happened."

He lifted her from where she was sitting on the fallen tree and she didn't object. She knew her feet wouldn't carry her a single step farther.

"I'll get you to hold the flashlight," Mr. Boone said. "Just shine it on the path a few feet in front of us."

She did, and they started back in the direction from which Mr. Boone had come.

"I'm not even going to worry about you dropping me," she said. "I'm too tired to care."

"I won't drop you," Mr. Boone said. "So don't you worry about that."

She forced herself to concentrate on holding the flashlight properly.

"The whole town's looking for you," Mr. Boone said. "Not in the bush, though. Mostly down by the water. They think you drowned. Your daughter's beside herself."

She remembered what she'd told Lydia about going in for a swim. She pictured her shoes and socks on the beach by her empty chair.

"Oh dear," she said.

"That's what they think all right," Mr. Boone said. "But you're not drowned, are you? Not by a long sight."

"So the boy's all right then?" she asked again. "They found him, did they?"

Mr. Boone hesitated, then he said, "I don't believe he was ever lost, Mrs. I believe that when your daughter and her niece came back from their party, Lenny was in his chair at the beach. It was you who was missing."

"Oh dear," she said, trying to think how she could have made such a mistake, how she could have got so confused. Surely if the boy had been sitting in his chair, she would have seen him.

Mr. Boone was silent and Lydia's mother could hear him breathing.

"Whenever you need to rest," she said, "just put me down." She hoped he wouldn't, though.

"Like I said before, you're light as a feather. There's nothing to you."

She wished he hadn't said that. It was too close to being true.

They walked along the dark path, Mr. Boone breathing heavily.

It was very hard for Lydia's mother to stay awake. She tried to imagine herself an ancient explorer.

"Just imagine, Mr. Boone," she heard herself say, "that we are in the prow of a boat and I am holding the lantern. We are travelling very slowly, believing the world is flat and that at any time we could go over the edge."

"You're a funny one, Mrs.," he said.

"Try to imagine that," she said, even though she herself was having trouble. The flashlight beam bounced along the dirt path and Mr. Boone's arms felt very real where they held her.

"I can't imagine such a thing," he said.

Why could neither of them imagine it? They knew too much, she decided, to accept such a concrete premise.

"Can you imagine the opposite then?" she asked him. "Can you imagine walking forever, never getting to an end?"

"I don't think so," he said.

She couldn't either. She was simply too old for that. Well then, there was nothing else to think about.

"He'll be all right, the boy," Mr. Boone said. "Don't be worrying about the boy." He was breathing very heavily now, and Lydia's mother knew that talking was an effort.

"I'm not worried, Mr. Boone," she said.

The lights from the cabins up ahead came into view through the trees. For a brief moment she wished that Mr. Boone could carry her right on by, past the cabins, along the gentle curve of the earth's surface to somewhere else. But that was impossible now.

She braced herself. She knew she would be berated for her foolishness, for all the trouble she had caused everyone, and she decided she would be silent, deferring to confusion and old age. She would not say a single word, would not try to explain what had happened, what thoughts had overcome her common sense. It was so ordinary and distasteful to her, squawking like a gull with absolutely nothing to say.

Criminal

"How come you don't have a girlfriend, Dwayne?" Mrs. Fricke asked. "You're so cute, I thought for sure you'd have a girlfriend by now."

Dwayne was playing a game on one of the demonstration models and Mrs. Fricke was watching the monitor over his shoulder. The manager was out and there was no-one in the store but them. Mrs. Fricke, who was a good twenty years older than Dwayne and married to a man with a gambling problem, had never said anything like that to him before. He didn't know what it meant. It wasn't like they had a teasing or bantering kind of relationship.

"I have lots of girlfriends," Dwayne said. "I just don't want to settle down."

"Hummm," Mrs. Fricke said, as though she didn't quite believe him. Then later, when she was standing behind him at the Xerox machine, she said, "You have a nice little butt."

Dwayne pretended not to hear. It was embarrassing.

"When I was your age," she said, "I would have killed to get my hands on a nice little butt like that."

Dwayne wondered if Mrs. Fricke was coming on to him, and if she was, whether he was going to have to quit his job. It wasn't such a great job anyway. His commission cheques never amounted to what he thought they should.

He avoided Mrs. Fricke for the rest of the afternoon, although he found himself looking at her in a new way and wondering whether he did have an especially nice butt. He decided maybe he did, and with that decision came a feeling of anticipation.

Dwayne worked until nine, then went home and changed into jeans. He picked up some beer and drove to a house-warming party at a brand new high-rise. His highschool friend Steven had just been transferred to Ottawa and Dwayne thought this party would be a chance to catch up on what the old Hamilton crowd was up to. When he got there, though, Steven was too busy being a host to stop and talk.

Dwayne gathered that most of the party guests were people Steven knew from his financial consulting firm. They were all pretty well dressed considering it was a casual party, and they looked like they frequented tanning salons and health clubs. Dwayne felt out of place, although he did manage to join in a few conversations in the crowded living room. When anyone asked him what he did for a living, he said he was a computer programmer. He didn't want to say he sold IBM clones on commission.

Dwayne wandered into the apartment's little kitchen, where Steven was pulling a roaster full of gooey chicken wings out of the oven.

"How are you doing?" Steven asked him. "I'll take you around and introduce you to people in a minute, if you want."

"That's okay," Dwayne said. "I think I've met most of them already."

"Nice people, eh," Steven said. He dumped the chicken wings on a big ceramic platter and carried it into the living room.

Dwayne wondered why he'd been invited. Then he remembered that he hadn't exactly been invited. He'd called Steven in the middle of the week to ask him if he wanted to go to a movie on Friday night and Steven had said he couldn't because he was having a house-warming, then he'd suggested that Dwayne drop by. Dwayne wished he hadn't.

There was an apartment-sized table with two chairs in the kitchen, and sitting on one of the chairs was a young woman who looked about as out of place as Dwayne felt. He watched her braid and unbraid a little piece of her long hair and then chug-a-lug most of a bottle of beer. She was wearing a sweatshirt with Hard Rock Café, New York on the front. Dwayne usually avoided conversations with women who looked like they didn't have a friend in the world. He was too afraid that would turn out to be true, and if it was there was bound to be a good reason. He spoke to this woman, though. Accidentally. She was wearing a name tag and he was reading her name to himself when it came to his lips and was out before he could stop it. Rachelle was her name, or at least that's what was on her name tag, and she didn't correct him when he said it out loud. All of a sudden he was sitting in the other chair, relieved to be talking to someone who didn't play squash at lunch hour. Not that he had anything against squash, but it wasn't fun to be so obviously an outsider.

"I'm not having a good time here," Rachelle said. "But I don't want to go home."

"Why is that?" Dwayne asked.

"Somebody set fire to the town house next to mine this morning. My neighbour called me at work. She said my basement's full of water from the fire trucks and my furniture's ruined from the smoke."

"You haven't been home yet?" Dwayne asked. He was thinking a fire in your town house was definitely enough to make you sit alone and play with your hair. He liked the Hard Rock Café sweatshirt, even though it was probably considered tacky by most of the people at Steven's party.

"No," Rachelle said. "I don't want to go home."

"I guess that explains why you're wearing the name tag," Dwayne said. "Because you haven't been home yet."

Rachelle took the tag off. "I work at a furniture store," she said. "We have to wear name tags so it looks like we're user friendly. It's one of those modular places. The stuff's all precut and drilled, you just have to screw it together. You know the kind I mean? It's real shitty furniture. Don't buy any."

Dwayne watched her turn the name tag over and over in her hand.

"So what are you going to do?" he asked.

"About what?"

"About your town house. You have to go home sometime, don't you?"

"I thought I'd just stay away until the water evaporates or something," Rachelle said. "I don't know. What do you think I should do?"

Dwayne didn't know. "I guess you could rent a sump pump," he said.

"I thought about leaving town," Rachelle said. "I can sell shitty furniture anywhere. It doesn't have to be in Ottawa."

"I wouldn't mind moving to B.C.," Dwayne said. "Kelowna might be nice."

"Yeah," Rachelle said. "Kelowna. That's where I'd like to go."

Rachelle drank two more beer, and then Dwayne offered to go home with her and see how much damage had been done. They took her car, which Dwayne drove because Rachelle had had too much to drink. On the way, he asked her if she'd been to the Hard Rock Café in New York.

"Fuckin' eh rights," she said.

"What were you doing at that party anyway?" Dwayne asked.

"I'm Steven's cousin," Rachelle said. "He was staying with me until he could find an apartment."

"Oh yeah," Dwayne said. "He mentioned he was staying with a relative."

"That was me," Rachelle said. "We didn't get along that well. We were kind of at each other's throats."

"Are you from Ottawa?" Dwayne asked.

"No way," Rachelle said. "I'm from the prairie, right smack in the middle."

"The prairie," Dwayne said. "Cowboys and Indians and all that."

"I came to Ottawa with a guy," Rachelle said, "but it didn't work out."

She directed him to where she lived, a subdivision with block after block of long, two-storey cedar buildings that had probably been fashionable twenty years ago, but now displayed all the telltale signs of low-grade building materials. The dark wooden structures looked like tinderboxes.

"There have been lots of fires around here lately," Rachelle said after they'd parked in front of her building. Dwayne leaned across the front seat of the car and kissed her.

"I'm really drunk," she said.

"That's okay," Dwayne said. He wanted her badly. He kissed her again and he knew she wasn't going to say no. They got out of the car.

"Arson, they think," Rachelle said. "Kids probably."

Dwayne noticed the boarded-up front window next to Rachelle's. "It's a wonder the whole block didn't go up," he said.

The front door on the other side of Rachelle's unit opened and a woman in a turquoise housecoat came out on her step.

"Oh God," Rachelle whispered. "This woman is incredible. She's been watching out the window for me. I don't believe it."

"I've been watching for you, dear," the woman called. "I thought you'd be home before now."

"I got held up," Rachelle said.

"It's a real mess. Don't be too upset when you see it."

"I brought a friend with me," Rachelle said, leaning a little on Dwayne to steady her walk.

"You're to call the cleaning company first thing in the morning," the woman said. "Insurance will pay. Of course, if you'd called today, you'd have had it taken care of sooner."

As Rachelle and Dwayne moved up the walk, the woman stepped down a step, as though wanting to get closer.

"The police caught the little bastards," she reported, leaning toward them, lowering her voice. "They threw a firebomb through Mrs. Perry's front window. Just for fun, if you can imagine that. They could have burned her up. Her place is gutted, you know. Completely gutted. Well. They caught them and I hope they throw the book at them." She paused and pulled her housecoat tightly around herself. "They can hang them for all I care," she said.

"I'm sure they'll get what's coming to them," Rachelle said. She pressed against Dwayne as they climbed the front steps.

"Do you want me to come in with you, dear?" the woman asked. It was obvious she was dying to get inside and have a look.

"No thanks," Rachelle said. "I've got my friend to help me out."

Dwayne could feel the woman watching them as Rachelle opened the door. They stepped inside, and Dwayne quickly locked the door again. They could smell the flooded basement and the acrid wood smoke.

"I wouldn't want to be her enemy," Dwayne said after the door was locked.

"She's okay," Rachelle said. "Just nosy is all."

"Should we have a look around?" Dwayne asked, although he

wasn't really thinking about the state of her town house.

"Never mind," Rachelle said. "Leave it until tomorrow." She had her hands on his hips and was pulling him to her. He kissed her, slid his hands up under the Hard Rock Café sweatshirt. He felt hot, like the place might still be burning somewhere. He was completely overcome.

Dwayne watched Mrs. Fricke's face closely when he told her he was moving to Kelowna with his girlfriend. He didn't know what he was watching for, exactly. Disappointment, maybe, but she didn't look disappointed at all. She looked delighted.

"I knew it wouldn't be long before some girl snapped you up," Mrs. Fricke said. "I hope you stay together for a long time and have a nice life." Then she asked, "How long have you known her anyway? Have you been keeping secrets?"

"Yeah," Dwayne lied. "I didn't want to tell anyone until I was sure we were … you know, serious."

"Well, she's a lucky girl," Mrs. Fricke said, and Dwayne found himself feeling a little disappointed that Mrs. Fricke was evidently not going to miss him.

Rachelle did most of the organizing to leave. She thought they should sell her car because Dwayne's was two years newer, so she advertised it in the paper and got what she wanted for it almost right away. She also advertised a fire sale and sold all her extra possessions, along with some of Dwayne's, on the lawn of the town house. She didn't have any trouble getting her damage deposit back, the landlord hadn't even bothered checking because of the smoke and water damage from the fire. Rachelle said that she was lucky to get the money because there was some damage from a party she'd had once. Some guy she didn't even know had fallen into the living room wall and put a hole in the plaster with his head. If it weren't for the fire, Rachelle would definitely have been out the deposit. She told Dwayne she was going to pull another fast one too, by leaving without paying her hydro or telephone bills. He said she'd never get hooked up again if she didn't pay them, but Rachelle said she was never moving back to Ontario anyway. Then she talked Dwayne into stealing something from the computer store to get the manager back for not paying him his commission. It was only fair, she said.

On Dwayne's last day of work, when he was alone in the store over the lunch hour, Rachelle came by and picked up a new laptop computer, still in its box. Dwayne hoped it would look, to anyone who happened to be watching, like she'd bought it. He was still sweating when he got home after work. He told Rachelle he'd been on the verge of a heart attack all afternoon, but she just laughed at him and said they could hock it in some town between Ottawa and Kelowna and they'd never get caught. Dwayne asked her why she was such an easy criminal. She told him it was because she had no fingerprints. She showed him and, to Dwayne's eye at least, it looked like the tips of her fingers were smooth.

"Contrary to what they tell you in school," Rachelle said, "it is possible to be born without fingerprints."

Dwayne didn't know whether to believe her or not. Accepting that a person could be born without fingerprints would be throwing open to question all kinds of things he'd been told, like no two snowflakes are alike.

"Anyway," Rachelle said, rubbing together the tips of her fingers, "don't worry about it. I'm not a murderer or anything. Compared to my brother Al, who has all his fingerprints, I'm not much of a criminal."

"You have a brother?" Dwayne asked.

"Unfortunately," Rachelle said. "And if you're lucky, you'll never have to spend Christmas with him."

It was late May and the cross-country trip seemed like an adventure. Dwayne owned a two-man nylon tent and they decided to camp even though they knew it would be cold. Rachelle had the car pretty well packed when Dwayne got home from work on his last day so they could get up early the next morning and leave. Dwayne didn't ask her what she'd done with the computer, although he assumed it was hidden somewhere in the car, under their clothes and the camping gear.

Late that night Dwayne realized he hadn't told Steven they were leaving. He phoned and got him out of bed.

"Hey, Dwayne," Steven said. "You can't call me like this. I've got to be fresh for work. I've got to make an impression."

"This is important," Dwayne said, and then he told Steve what he and Rachelle were doing. There was silence on Steven's end of the line.

"Aren't you going to say anything?" Dwayne asked.

"You've only known each other for two weeks," Steven said.

"Yeah, but bells and whistles went off," Dwayne said.

"All I can think of to say is good luck," Steven said.

"Thanks buddy," Dwayne said. "We'll send you an address card when we get settled."

After he hung up the phone, Dwayne thought maybe there was something wrong. Steven hadn't sounded his usual enthusiastic self. Then he decided it was because Steven had been half asleep.

They were on the highway by sun-up the next morning. Dwayne felt reckless and elated. He thought Rachelle had changed his life, pulled him out of the rut of a boring job and an ordinary future. He couldn't believe that he was heading across the country with stolen goods, just like a real criminal. He wished his car were a convertible so they could drive with the top down. He wanted to see Rachelle's hair blowing in the wind.

They put in a long day of driving and spent the first night in a campground near a town called Marathon. The campground was deserted except for them, the attendant and a dog, which the attendant told them was a stray. The dog looked well-enough fed, and Dwayne could see why because it knew how to endear itself to people. It hung around them while they were setting up the tent, wagging its tail and holding up one paw for a shake. For supper, they heated canned beef stew over the fire, and they gave the dog a whole can for himself. Afterward, they went for a walk along the shore of Lake Superior and the dog went with them, bounding ahead but always returning to make sure they were still there.

"This is a nice dog," Dwayne said to the attendant when they got back to the campground. "How come nobody's taken him home?"

"That dog's the best actor I've ever come across," the attendant said, laughing. "He's pretending to be your dog. I've seen him do it a thousand times. Just try and get him in your car and see what happens."

They walked back to their campsite. The dog followed them and lay down right in front of the tent flap. It was getting cold. Dwayne said he was ready to hit the sack, but Rachelle decided she wanted to find a bar and have a few beers.

"Really?" Dwayne said.

"Don't you?" Rachelle asked.

"Sure," Dwayne said, "if you do." He was thinking that this was northern Ontario and you could run into some pretty tough characters in a bar, but then he remembered he was reckless and he said, "Yeah. Let's go. I'm game."

Just for fun, Dwayne tried to get the dog into the car with them. The dog wouldn't budge from his spot in front of the tent. Dwayne even tried to lure him into the car with sandwich meat, but the dog wasn't in the least interested.

"Forget it," Rachelle said. "He likes his freedom. He's an itinerant dog."

"It doesn't make sense," Dwayne said. "He could be fat and happy with us. He'd never have to worry about a thing."

"It's just occurred to me," Rachelle said, "that you are a real dreamer." She said it in an indifferent kind of way and Dwayne couldn't quite tell if she meant it or not. He didn't think he was a dreamer.

The bar they found was surprisingly quiet. Dwayne tried to have a good time but he was tired from driving, had a headache, in fact. He nursed one beer so long it got warm. Rachelle drank three or four to his one, and kept saying things like, "You sure like to get your money's worth out of one beer, don't you?" He thought she might be annoyed with him, but then he thought she was teasing. They played a few games of pool and headed back to the campground. Dwayne assumed the dog would be waiting for them, but he wasn't. They zipped their sleeping bags together and tried to get warm enough to fall asleep.

When they were lying in the dark, both of them wearing T-shirts and socks because they were so cold, Rachelle said, "Where did you get the name Dwayne anyway? No-one's called Dwayne anymore." He had no answer except, "It's what my mother called me." That seemed to satisfy her and she went to sleep, but Dwayne couldn't. He was hurt that she called him a dreamer and now she didn't like his name. It seemed as if she was picking on him. He finally fell asleep, but in the early morning he woke up with the sun shining through the tent walls and he thought about Rachelle not liking his name again, and then he started thinking that they should have sold his car instead of Rachelle's, because if his old boss discovered he had one less laptop computer than he should have, he might put two and two together. He'd give Dwayne's name to the police and they'd be able to trace him through his car licence number. He worried about it until Rachelle woke up, and when he told her they'd made a mistake with the cars she told him to relax, even if his boss did miss the computer, he wouldn't call the police on Dwayne because Dwayne would tell them about the unpaid commission money.

"It's tit for tat," Rachelle said. "Relax and enjoy yourself."

"I don't see why you said that about my name last night," Dwayne said to her.

She sat up and looked at him. Her hair was all messy and Dwayne thought it was sexy. Through the tent wall he could see the shadow of the stray dog sniffing around.

"Have you got hurt feelings?" Rachelle asked.

"Maybe," Dwayne said.

"Hurt feelings are for babies," Rachelle said. Then she climbed on top of him and guided his already hard penis inside of her. Dwayne closed his eyes and forgot about his hurt feelings. He let Rachelle take him to a dangerous and unfamiliar place, where his bones melted away so that he couldn't move and he was held together by her body wrapped around his.

About the time they passed through Thunder Bay, Dwayne noticed Rachelle playing with her hair, looking distracted or maybe worried about something. When he asked her what was wrong, she said she supposed there was no way they could avoid Regina, her old home town.

"It's right on the Number One highway," she said. "Just sitting there like a giant roadblock."

"You don't want to stop and call anybody up?" Dwayne asked.

"We could take the bypass and not go into the city at all," Rachelle said. "That way I wouldn't have to see much of it. I could watch it in the rear-view mirror."

"If you want," Dwayne said. "I'm not crazy about the idea of driving in a strange city anyway."

"If we stopped," Rachelle said, "we'd have to stay with my mother."

"We can stop if you want to," Dwayne said. "It's completely up to you."

"You wouldn't want to meet my mother," Rachelle said. "Or my brother either, but there's not much chance of that, unless you feel like going out to the jail."

"Not with a stolen computer in the back of the car," Dwayne said. "No thanks."

He wondered what kind of family Rachelle came from, and thought about how scandalized his own mother would be if she knew he was driving across Canada with stolen goods in the car. His mother, who still lived in Hamilton, was so scrupulously honest that she sent money to the War Amps when they mailed her her personalized key tags, even though she didn't want them.

"What can you do?" she said. "They don't want them back, and you can't keep them without paying for them. Every time I looked at them I'd think they were stolen."

All day long Rachelle wavered back and forth as to whether or not they should stop. Finally, late in the afternoon, she said, "I don't think we should stop. There. It's decided. Now I feel better."

"Fine," Dwayne said. "We'll just breeze on past." He was satisfied that the decision had been made. He thought, though, that he'd seen something new in Rachelle, a crack that had started early in the day and had grown wider as they got farther west. He felt vindicated for the mean things she'd said to him the night before. He felt a kind of anticipation building, like when Mrs. Fricke told him he had a nice butt.

They stopped at Kenora that night, just on the Ontario side of the provincial border. Rachelle said she didn't want to stay in a campground again, she wanted wilderness and the great outdoors without showers and laundrettes and motor homes for neighbours. Dwayne pointed out that it was so early in the season the campgrounds were empty, but Rachelle wouldn't be swayed. They bought a dozen beer, then drove out of town to a spot along the lake and parked the car under a sign that said Positively No Camping, which made Dwayne more than a little nervous, but Rachelle said park wardens weren't the same as police. They left everything in the car and hiked along the lake shore until Rachelle picked a spot where she wanted to camp. Then they went back to the car for the tent and the beer. Dwayne insisted on taking the computer out of the car and hiding it in the bush in case the police came along and searched the car during the night. Rachelle told him he was being paranoid.

"You're supposed to camp in the campground," Dwayne said as they were setting up the tent. "This is against the law. We shouldn't be doing things against the law until we've hocked that computer."

"I'm not worried," Rachelle said. "Are you?"

"I'm not really worried," Dwayne said. "I just don't think we're being very smart."

"If you're worried we can go to a campground."

"I'm not worried," Dwayne said. "I didn't say I was worried."

"If we use dry wood for the fire it won't smoke much," Rachelle said. "If that makes you feel any better."

"You don't have to talk like I'm worried about it," Dwayne said. "I told you I'm not worried."

Rachelle looked at him like she didn't believe him. Dwayne got the feeling she was enjoying his uneasiness, which made him want to argue with her, but then she'd be more convinced he was uneasy so he let it drop.

They made a fire and drank the beer. The sun went down and it grew dark and quiet. The air smelled of evergreens. Dwayne decided he was hungry.

"We should have brought some food with us," he said.

"Do you want to go back to town?" Rachelle asked.

"Do you?" Dwayne asked.

"I can wait until morning."

"I can too then," Dwayne said.

Rachelle pulled a joint out of her purse. Dwayne was annoyed because he'd said he didn't want to travel with any dope in the car and at the time Rachelle had agreed. She assured him the joint was all she'd brought and they smoked it. Dwayne couldn't stop thinking about food. Finally he decided to drive to town and pick up a burger. Rachelle didn't want to go and said she'd stay and keep the fire going.

"I don't think you should stay here alone," Dwayne said.

"What could happen?" Rachelle asked.

"Bears. Wolves. I don't know. Anything could happen."

"I'm not scared," Rachelle said.

So Dwayne went, taking a flashlight with him so he could find his way to the car and back.

When he returned an hour later, the fire had died down and Rachelle was nowhere to be seen. Dwayne looked in the tent, called softly, but there was no answer. He walked to the water's edge and tried to look up and down the shoreline for her, but the moon was hidden by clouds and he couldn't see a thing. He didn't know what to do. He built the fire up again so she'd see it, then he walked down to the lake with the flashlight and shone it out over the water. He shouted her name, but his own voice disappearing into the dark scared him. He went back and stood by the fire, fluctuating between panic and reason. One moment, he'd believe the worst had happened, that she'd gone for a swim in the frigid water and drowned. Then he'd relax and tell himself she'd just gone for a walk along the shore, and that any second she was going to walk into the light of the fire as though nothing was wrong. He looked at his watch. It was eleven-thirty. He'd wait until midnight, he decided, and if she hadn't shown up by then he'd drive to the police station and report her missing. He sat on a rock by the fire. A breeze came across the lake and blew smoke and heat in his eyes.

Thinking about going to the police station panicked him again. He convinced himself the police had issued a Canada-wide warrant for his arrest. He'd walk into the police station to report Rachelle missing and they'd charge him on the spot with theft. Not petty theft either. Serious theft. He never should have let her talk him into stealing the computer. She was different from him. She had a criminal mind, he thought. She wasn't even worried about getting caught. He grew angry with her, for making him steal the computer and for disappearing in the middle of nowhere. He looked at his watch again. It was twenty to twelve. Maybe he wouldn't report her missing. Maybe he'd wait until morning and then he'd just leave if she hadn't shown up. Immediately, though, his fear and anger were replaced by guilt for even considering leaving her. He opened another beer, then sat back on the rock again, trying to get control of himself.

"Dway-ane," a voice said from the bush behind him.

Dwayne jumped up, spilling his beer, and faced the black line of trees. He listened.

"Dway-ane," the voice came again.

"Rachelle?" Dwayne said, unable to stop his voice from trembling. "Is that you?"

"No," the voice said. "It's the camping police and I've come to arrest you."

"Jesus Christ, Rachelle," Dwayne said, throwing down his beer bottle. It hit a rock and broke. "You scared the shit out of me. Get the fuck out here right now."

Dwayne heard dead wood cracking not twenty feet from where he was standing and Rachelle emerged from the darkness. She wasn't laughing, which made the game seem even more cruel.

"How could you do that to me?" Dwayne asked. He wanted to grab her and shake her. It was all he could do to stop himself. "I thought you were dead," he said.

"You thought I was dead?" Rachelle asked. "How could I be dead?"

"I thought you'd drowned," Dwayne said. Then he said, "I thought you loved me. How could you do that to me if you loved me?"

Rachelle looked away from him, toward the lake.

"I never said I loved you," she said.

"I know you didn't say it," Dwayne said. "But I thought you did. I thought that was why we were going to Kelowna together."

"Let's go swimming," Rachelle said.

"Don't be crazy," Dwayne said.

"It'll be cold," Rachelle said. "But we can do it. It will make us remember this spot forever." She was already taking off her clothes.

"I'm not going in swimming, Rachelle," Dwayne said. "You might be stupid enough to do that, but I'm not."

"You better come with me," Rachelle said. "I can't swim." She started walking toward the lake.

"Don't go in that water, Rachelle," Dwayne said.

She kept walking.

"When you're dead, you're dead, you know," Dwayne shouted. She didn't even turn to look at him. It was as though she was certain he would come. Either that, or she was daring him not to. He watched her step into the water, watched her white body rapidly disappear ahead of him as the lake bottom dropped away.

He took off his clothes and walked down to the water. He couldn't see her anymore, but he could hear little splashes out in front of him.

"You have to do this with conviction," Rachelle said from the darkness. "Otherwise, you won't do it."

Dwayne stepped in. The rocks hurt his feet, but he hardly noticed because the water was so cold on his ankles. He couldn't believe that anything could live in that water. He walked in up to his knees, but then he had to stop. He couldn't bring himself to go any farther. His ankles and calves were aching and the darkness made him feel disoriented.

He was about to turn and go back when he lost his balance and staggered forward. The lake bottom dropped away from him and his chest hit the frigid water. He couldn't breathe. He tried to regain his footing, but he couldn't find the bottom. He couldn't even call for help because he couldn't breathe out, his chest just kept sucking air. He thought he was going to drown, even though he was only fifteen feet from the shore. Then he found the bottom, and somehow he started breathing again. The water was up to his shoulders. He saw Rachelle gliding toward him, swimming. She swam right up to him and wrapped her legs around him. Her teeth were chattering and when she pressed herself against him, her body felt icy cold.

"Do you love me?" she asked.

He didn't even have to think about it. The answer was no. He didn't love her, and he didn't want her cold body against him. He wanted to push her away.

"Let's get the fuck out of this lake," he said. "There's an iceberg in it somewhere."

"I knew you didn't," she said. "So don't start throwing that 'I thought you loved me' stuff around. I'm too smart for that."

They had no towels so they had to stand in the heat of the fire until they were dry. Even when Dwayne was standing practically on top of the fire, he could feel the ice in his bones. After they were in their sleeping bags Rachelle said, "Anyway, how could you love me? You don't even know me." Dwayne didn't answer. He had never been so cold in his entire life. He shivered all night, and he could feel Rachelle shivering too.

"I guess we'll make it to Regina today," Rachelle said the next morning. They were having breakfast at an Esso on the highway, both of them with their hands wrapped around hot cups of coffee. "Maybe I should call my mother from a phone booth. Just to let her know I'm still alive."

Dwayne looked at Rachelle across the table. He didn't know what had happened the night before. He felt like something had been exposed, but he wasn't sure what it was. He knew that, whatever it was, they weren't going to talk about it. He noticed Rachelle was wearing the Hard Rock Café sweatshirt.

"We might as well stop overnight," he said. The words escaped from his lips the way Rachelle's name had when he first met her.

"I don't want to stop," Rachelle said. "I don't even want to call her. It's just that I think I should."

"I want to meet your mother," Dwayne said. "You don't have to worry about anything. I'll be there."

"I hate my mother," Rachelle said. "Don't be surprised when you see that."

They paid their breakfast bill and headed west into Manitoba, each of them with a Styrofoam cup of hot coffee, the computer once again stowed in the hatchback.

"Did you like New York?" Dwayne asked Rachelle.

"What?" Rachelle asked, apparently not understanding his question.

"New York," Dwayne said, pointing to her sweatshirt. "Did you like it?"

"Oh that," Rachelle said. "I bought it at a garage sale. I wouldn't go to New York if you paid me."

They pulled up to Rachelle's mother's house in the early evening. Dwayne guessed that this was the kind of neighbourhood where young professional couples bought old houses cheap and fixed them up. Most of the houses on the block looked newly renovated. They were painted trendy colours like dove grey or California peach.

Rachelle's mother's house, a two-storey stucco, was so badly in need of repair it stuck out. Dwayne noticed that the houses on either side of it had For Sale signs on the lawns, and he could imagine the owners worrying about property value.

"You'd better move the car ahead a bit," Rachelle said. "She'll tie into you for parking in her spot."

Dwayne did.

"She won't be home for a while," Rachelle said as they walked up to the front door. "She works until midnight." She stopped and stared. "Jesus," she said. "Look at that."

Rachelle was looking at an old wooden barrel on the step just outside the front door. A chain had been fed through two holes in the barrel and then padlocked to the rusted cast iron handrail.

"There you go," Rachelle said. "Now you've met my mother."

Two small dogs began to bark wildly on the other side of the door and Rachelle pushed them inside as she unlocked the door and opened it.

"They're horrible dogs," she told Dwayne. "They bite."

The dogs wagged their tails hesitantly for Rachelle, and looked at Dwayne with suspicion.

"What are their names?" he asked.

"Muffy and Fudge," Rachelle said. She turned to him. "Let's just leave," she said. "I hate these fucking dogs. I forgot how much I hate these dogs."

"They're not so bad," Dwayne said. He held out his hand. "Here Muffy. Here Fudge." Both dogs snarled.

"Get away," Rachelle said, kicking at them. They turned tail, as though they were used to that.

Rachelle took Dwayne upstairs to her old bedroom overlooking the street. It was hot and stuffy and Dwayne opened the window. The bedroom was small, furnished with an old iron bed, once painted white, now chipped and peeling. There was an old dresser, also in need of paint, and a worn pink carpet on the floor.

"It's not such a bad room," Dwayne said. "I'll carry our things up."

"I think we should go to a hotel," Rachelle said.

"Don't be stupid," Dwayne said, he wasn't sure why. He was excited about being in the house and he didn't understand it. "A hotel costs money," he said. "Your mother's house is free."

He took their bags upstairs while Rachelle stood around looking morose. Dwayne found some Campbell's soup in the cupboard and bologna in the fridge for sandwiches. They were watching a late movie on TV, or at least pretending to watch, when Rachelle's mother pulled up in front of the house. Rachelle recognized the sound of the car. Dwayne looked out the window and saw a squat, grey-haired woman get out of an old black Charger. The passenger side door was green, obviously a replacement from another vehicle.

"It's Al's car," Rachelle said without getting up. "In the summer he rides a motorcycle. Anyway, he's in jail now so he won't be needing either one."

Rachelle's mother was staring at the strange car in front of the house, studying the licence plate as though she were memorizing the number. She was wearing some kind of paramilitary uniform.

"What does your mother do for a living?" Dwayne asked.

"She's a night security guard at some office building," Rachelle said. "Just thank God they don't allow her to carry a gun."

"Aren't you going to meet her at the door?" Dwayne asked.

Rachelle didn't move.

"Come on, Rachelle," he said. "Get up. She's your mother."

Dwayne was lying on top of Rachelle's bed waiting for her when he heard them arguing in the hallway at the foot of the stairs.

"Are you going to see Al?" Rachelle's mother was asking.

"No," Rachelle said.

"You should go and see him," her mother said. "He's your brother."

"I'm not going to see him," Rachelle said.

"He's paying his debt," Rachelle's mother said. "Which is more than I can say for some people."

"I don't owe anybody anything," Rachelle said.

"I don't know why you bothered to stop."

"I don't know why either. Dwayne wanted to. It was his idea."

"Well, if you feel that way you might as well leave right now. Why don't you just get in the car and go right now."

Dwayne got up and went to the top of the stairs.

"Rachelle?" he called. "Come to bed, honey." He didn't know why he called her honey. He'd never called her that before. Rachelle's mother's grey face peered up at him from the bottom of the stairs, an ugly face, worn and distrustful.

"Rachelle's tired," Dwayne said to her. "We drove all day. And we didn't get much sleep last night."

"Mind your own business, Dwayne," Rachelle shouted at him.

"You make her go and see her brother tomorrow," Rachelle's mother said to Dwayne. "And tell her she can't leave right away. That's a fine way to treat your family."

"Come to bed, Rachelle," Dwayne said.

Rachelle pushed her way past her mother and stomped up the stairs. "Just stay out of my business, Dwayne," she said to him. Dwayne followed her into the bedroom, where she flopped down on her stomach on top of the bed. At first he thought she was crying, but then he saw she wasn't.

"Okay," he said. "I'm sorry. We can leave in the morning. It doesn't make any difference to me."

Rachelle said nothing.

"What did Al do anyway?" Dwayne asked.

"How should I know," Rachelle said. "B and E. Trafficking. How should I know."

Dwayne looked around the room. "Where's your old stuff?" he asked. "Shouldn't there be dolls and stuffed animals and movie star pictures on the dresser?"

"You don't know what you've done by making us stop here," Rachelle said.

"I'd hardly say I made us stop," Dwayne said. "It was you who brought it up in the first place."

"Don't ever call me honey again," she said. "That's such shit."

The next morning while Rachelle was still in bed, her mother whined to Dwayne. She was no longer wearing her security guard uniform. Now she was wearing a man's cotton knit golf shirt and shiny old dress pants cinched at the waist with a belt. She was so thoroughly unattractive that Dwayne didn't want to look at her, but several times he caught himself staring. She didn't seem to notice.

Her whining went on and on. She told Dwayne that since Al had gone to jail there'd been nobody to do anything around the house. She made Dwayne go outside with her and pointed out all the things that had to be done. The storm windows needed to be taken off. The roof needed new shingles. The front lawn was still covered with last year's leaves. She complained about the neighbours' cats. She'd set a cat trap in her yard, she said, and one of the neighbours had circulated a flyer about it up and down both sides of the street. She told Dwayne her life had been threatened since that happened. She'd had phone calls telling her if she didn't get rid of the cat trap she'd be sorry. So she'd got rid of it and now the neighbours' cats were destroying her yard. She'd been persecuted, and there was no one to defend her. She'd called the police but they hadn't done a thing.

"I try to keep the house up," Rachelle's mother told him, "but what can I do, a woman alone? I get no help. The neighbours do nothing for me, my son is in jail, my daughter only thinks about herself. I don't know how I keep going. The dogs help. They're good watch dogs, you know. I wouldn't feel safe in my own house if it weren't for the dogs."

Dwayne got depressed because he couldn't think of a way to excuse himself. He was stuck following her around the yard. He didn't want to reshingle her roof, or clean up rotten leaves from the lawn. He did that kind of thing for his own mother when he went home, but he didn't want to do any favours for this woman, who he knew would be ungrateful. Rachelle's mother led him back to the front of the house and pointed to the wooden barrel chained to the front step.

"Take that barrel," she said. "I found that barrel over a year ago and I've been planning to saw it in half so I can plant geraniums in it. Do you think I can get anyone to do that for me?"

She stood at the foot of the steps, hands on her hips, and looked at Dwayne. Dwayne knew he was supposed to say he would do it.

"Three times I've caught someone trying to steal it," she said. "The last time it was them." She pointed to the house next door, and Dwayne thought he knew why it had the For Sale sign on the lawn.

"These barrels are not easy to come by," Rachelle's mother said. "You see them in magazines nowadays. People give their eye teeth for them. But they're no good unless you've got someone to cut them in half for you."

Dwayne made up his mind he was not going to cut the barrel in half. He saw Rachelle in the front doorway and waited for her to say it was time for them to leave.

"Saw the barrel in half for her, Dwayne," she said. She sounded tired.

"No," Dwayne said. "I won't."

"Thanks," Rachelle said. "Thanks a lot."

"What do you mean?" Dwayne asked. "It's got nothing to do with you, for Christ's sake."

At that moment a boy about ten years old came from across the street toward them. He headed for the next-door neighbour's house and put a key in the front door lock. Rachelle's mother strode across the lawn and up the neighbour's walk after him.

"What are you doing?" she barked at the boy.

"I'm going in to feed the rabbit," he said.

"Did they tell you to do that?"

"They gave me a key. I'm supposed to do it."

Dwayne could tell the boy was frightened.

"Go home," Rachelle's mother said to him. The boy was standing on the front step, the key still in the lock. He didn't move. Dwayne couldn't believe what he was seeing. The boy was obviously too afraid to move.

"Go on," Rachelle's mother said, waving her arms. "Go on home. I'll feed the rabbit. I'm the next-door neighbour."

The boy ran. Rachelle's mother pulled the door shut again and stuck the key in her pants pocket. She walked back across the lawn and into her own house, ignoring Dwayne and Rachelle. She came out a minute later with a handful of lettuce leaves, which she took next door.

"She has no idea," Rachelle said. "She doesn't have a clue."

Rachelle didn't make any move to pack her things. At noon Dwayne saw that her nightgown was still lying on top of the unmade bed. Her toothbrush was in the bathroom and the Hard Rock Café sweatshirt was inside out on the floor next to her suitcase, where she'd dropped it the night before. He didn't know whether to say anything to her or not.

After lunch Rachelle went somewhere with her mother in Al's Charger and Dwayne had to wait for them to come back. He thought they were probably going to see Al. He wondered if he should just cut the barrel in half and be done with it, but then he thought damned if he was going to do that, and then he thought maybe he should just get in the car and leave. That took him back to when he was going to leave Rachelle in the bush when he assumed she was lost, only this time the desire to leave her was stronger. He had another attack of guilt.

He went upstairs to Rachelle's bedroom and thought about the sorry state of the chipped furniture. He decided to paint it. He drove around until he found a strip mall with a hardware store, and he bought some white enamel and a brush. Painting the bed and dresser kept him busy for a couple of hours, but when he finished Rachelle and her mother still weren't home. He got in the car again and went back to the mall. He bought Rachelle a big stuffed panda for a present.

When he returned, Rachelle was sitting on the step by the barrel. Dwayne got out of the car with the panda and asked her if she wanted to head for Kelowna again even though it was late in the day. She told him she wasn't going.

"When I saw the car wasn't here," she said, "I thought you'd already gone. I was hoping you had."

Dwayne handed her the panda.

"I bought this for you," he said. He was thinking she might not accept it. She took it, though, and told Dwayne she would think up a good name for it because she had named all of her stuffed animals when she was a child.

Dwayne woke in the night to the sound of a handsaw rasping back and forth. The sound was coming from right under the open second-storey window. He got up and looked outside.

"Jesus Christ," he said in the darkness. "Do you know what your mother is doing?"

"She's sawing the barrel in half," Rachelle said.

"Jesus. Does she have to do that in the middle of the night?"

Rachelle didn't answer and Dwayne got back into bed, lying on top of the sheets. It was hot and the room smelled of fresh paint. He thought he should feel sorrier than he did that Rachelle wasn't coming with him in the morning. He rolled over toward her and tried to put his arm around her.

"Don't," she said. "It's too hot."

He lay on his back, relieved, listening to the saw and smelling the paint.

"Your mother is crazy," he said.

"I told you I didn't want to stop," Rachelle said. "We'd be in Kelowna by now if you'd just kept on driving."

"Why do you think she's doing that?" Dwayne asked. He was talking about the barrel. "I mean, why now? She said herself it's been sitting on the step for over a year."

"She's doing it for you," Rachelle said. "If you haven't figured that out, you don't know much."

"I don't know why she's bothering," Dwayne said. "She'll never see me again."

Rachelle rolled over so her back was to Dwayne. "Al's getting out of jail," she said. "In a couple of weeks."

"Well, that's good news," Dwayne said.

"Yeah," Rachelle said. "Good news."

In the morning Dwayne carried his bag down to the car. Rachelle went with him as far as the step and sat down where the barrel used to be. The barrel was lying in two halves on the lawn.

"Do you think she'll plant geraniums in it?" Dwayne asked, doubting.

"She won't," Rachelle said. "I might. I don't mind doing things like that."

Dwayne didn't know whether to kiss her goodbye or not. He couldn't believe that something like this could end so quickly. He didn't know how he felt, only that he'd called her honey and now he was leaving without her. He thought maybe he should ask her if she'd like to keep the computer, but he didn't want to bring it up. It was embarrassing now, what they'd done together. In the end, he just said he'd send her a postcard when he had an address and she could join him whenever she felt like it. He was lying about the postcard, and he knew Rachelle knew it, but she didn't say anything and let him leave in a dignified way, for which he was grateful.

Dwayne drove through town until he hit the highway. At the junction it occurred to him that he didn't really have to go to Kelowna, he could go back east again, to Ottawa or even Hamilton. He decided, though, that he might as well keep going since he'd come this far.

When he was well outside the city, he turned off onto a grid road. He drove until he was out of sight of the highway traffic, then stopped and got the computer, still in its box, out of the hatchback. He threw it as far as he could into a farmer's field, but as soon it was out of his hands he started to worry that his fingerprints were on the box. He walked out to where it lay in the black earth and rubbed it all over with his jacket. After that was done he headed west again, a relatively free man, although he didn't feel good about his freedom and wouldn't for a long time.

The Way We Live

SYLVIA felt sorry for the dishwasher because he was young and good-looking and had something wrong with him. She knew there was something wrong with him because the cafeteria was run by a support organization for psychiatric patients. Everyone who worked there lived in a halfway house.

There was a window between the cafeteria and the kitchen, and every day Sylvia watched the dishwasher scrape leftover food from dirty dishes, and then dunk them into a huge stainless steel sink. It must be terrible to be a dishwasher, she thought. She began to sense his resentment at having to deal with other people's garbage. She tried to be courteous. She was careful to clean her own plate before she handed her tray through the window. Although he never smiled back, she always smiled at him when she caught his eye. She thought she was saying, "I understand. It would disgust me too."

Sylvia told Eddy about the dishwasher.

"I don't know why you're making a big deal out of this," he said. "The guy has a job as a dishwasher. Lots of people work as dishwashers."

"But this guy wouldn't if he wasn't screwed up," Sylvia said. "You can tell he'd be doing something else."

"You're romanticizing," Eddy said, fiddling with his cassette player. He was playing guitar scales over chord changes on a tape.

Sylvia went to the bedroom to find a pair of earrings. All her earrings, even the good ones, were in a pile on the dresser. It was next to impossible to find two that matched.

"You don't care about people," Sylvia said to Eddy. "It's because you sit around all day and smoke dope."

Eddy said nothing to defend himself.

The dishwasher handed Sylvia's plate back to her one day, saying, "You forgot something." Sylvia looked at her plate. There was nothing there. She was disconcerted by the fact that he had actually spoken to her and now she didn't know what to do.

"It looks like you chewed something up and spit it back out again," the dishwasher said. "It looks like a piece of chicken fat. Or maybe a pork chop. It's hard to tell now that it's all chewed up and mixed with spit."

Sylvia stared at her plate. She'd had a grilled cheese sandwich for lunch and all she could see was grease and a dab of ketchup.

"Oh for Christ's sake," the dishwasher said. "Give it to me. I don't have all day." He took the plate and scraped the imaginary food into the garbage.

Sylvia went back to work and worried about the bizarre incident all afternoon. She felt her neck flush every time she thought about it. She'd been embarrassed for herself, because she hadn't known how to handle the incident, and for him, because it was obvious he was still crazy. He was either hallucinating or his particular mental problem had to do with unnaturally aggressive behaviour. Maybe both. In either case, he shouldn't be working in a kitchen with knives. She considered telling the cafeteria supervisor about the episode, but soon realized she couldn't because of the intimacy of the details. She didn't want to talk about her own masticated food, even if it hadn't really been there. And the supervisor didn't seem very friendly. She was all business.

At the back of Sylvia's mind was the nagging possibility that the dishwasher had interpreted her smile as condescension. Perhaps she had been observing him too intently. Perhaps she had been staring. But she preferred to believe the problem lay with him. The result of the incident was that Sylvia ate in the cafeteria as seldom as possible and often walked to the Bay to shop instead.

At the Bay she met R. Sylvia was standing by the perfume counter, about to ask for free samples. She liked Obsession and had just used the last of her sample vial. R was standing at the counter next to her. She felt him looking at her and heard his voice say, "I especially like blonde hair." Her hair was blonde. She ignored him, but was thrown enough to actually purchase a small bottle of perfume, which she couldn't afford, instead of asking for the samples. He said, "Not only do I like blondes, but Obsession is my absolutely favourite scent on a woman." He was insistent. Sylvia found this just as disconcerting as the incident with the dishwasher, but she handled it better. This may have been because R was smiling and well-dressed and obviously not crazy. They had lunch. She gave him her phone number at work. They had lunch again. Pretty soon they were arranging to meet at R's friend's empty apartment. It was all very secretive because R was married and Sylvia was living with Eddy. It was definitely the beginning of what you would call an affair.

Before they made love for the first time, R questioned her about her sexual history. She took this as a sign of sophistication and told him she hadn't slept with anyone but Eddy since Aids had become an issue.

"What about him?" R asked. "Has he been faithful to you?"

"Of course," Sylvia said. Then she asked R about his past, not because she was worried, but because she wanted to be as sophisticated as he was.

He looked surprised, perhaps even a little insulted, but he quickly recovered and called her "kitten" and told her she had nothing to worry about. He told her how turned on he was by her blonde hair. He told her he knew sex with her was going to be special. When the time came to find out, though, Sylvia got the impression R was trying to do it without actually touching her. It wasn't very satisfying but she kept seeing him, she couldn't explain why. Maybe she liked having a secret from Eddy.

Eddy thought they should buy a car. Sylvia didn't want to.

"I guess it's up to you," Eddy said. "You're the one who makes the most money."

"You know I don't hold that over you," Sylvia said.

"I didn't mean it to sound that way," Eddy said. "I really do believe it's your decision. I just wanted to bring it up. We could go for drives in the country."

"Drives in the country. That's a strange notion." She had never actually been for a drive in the country. "You do that on Sunday afternoon, right?"

"Right," Eddy said. "It would be nice."

Sylvia supposed that drives in the country sounded all right, but she hadn't driven a car for so long she hadn't even renewed her licence. She'd probably have to take another test. And cars were bound to cost more than drives in the country were worth. She told Eddy they could probably borrow a car some nice weekend instead, if he wanted to be bothered driving.

One day Sylvia had to go to work without earrings because she could no longer sort out the tangled mess on her dresser. At noon, she bought seven pairs of fashion earrings on sale, dirt cheap, at the Bay. One pair cost only fifty cents. She wondered which pair of earrings to wear after work. She was meeting R at his cousin's apartment. His cousin was in Jamaica on business and R was looking after his cat.

She tried on all seven pairs in the washroom at work, and the decision was finally made for her when someone came in and wanted to use the mirror. Sylvia scooped the six pairs that were on the counter into her purse and left with three-inch pink plastic discs in her ears. She thought they looked good with her black turtleneck sweater. R hated them and made her throw them in the garbage. She didn't tell him about the other ones in her purse. He probably would have made her throw them out too.

When Sylvia got home, Eddy was sitting on his usual stool in the living room, playing scales. Smoke curled up from the joint he had impaled on the wild end of a guitar string.

"Jesus," Sylvia said to him. "Can't you get through one day without that crap?"

"I love my reefer," Eddy said. "You know that."

Between R and the Bay, Sylvia was down to eating about once a week in the cafeteria at work. She tried to watch the dishwasher without actually looking at him. He hates me, she thought.

One day Sylvia ran into Phil on a city bus. He was an old boyfriend from highschool and she'd liked him a lot, but that had been a long time ago in another town so she quickly looked away and tried to pretend she hadn't recognized him. Of course that didn't work. He was a very friendly person and was not at all embarrassed about running into someone from his past. He actually seemed glad to see her. Their conversation went like this.

"My God. Sylvia Chartrand."

"Phil. Phil James."

"Holy shit. Long time no see. Do you live here?"

"Yes. You?"

"Yeah. And we've never run into one another. It's not such a small world after all, eh. Well, well, well. Sylvia Chartrand. You married now?"

"I'm living with someone."

"Living with. Oh. I see. Well, how's that working out?"

"Fine. Good. It's a good arrangement. How about you?"

"Married. Thirteen years to the same woman. Pretty good, eh. Three kids. Great kids. God, I love kids."

"You still work on cars? I remember you used to love to work on old cars."

"I sell them now. For a living. Real cars. Buicks. Not those Japanese tin cans the consumer magazines push. Everyone thinks they're so great, but drive one into a telephone pole and you'll find out how great they are. So. What kind of car do you drive?"

"I don't have a car."

"No car? Christ, woman. This is the nineties. You should have at least two cars."

"I take the bus a lot."

"This is my first time. First time on a city bus. It's humiliating. I'm out for a test drive with this guy, eh, and I need smokes. So I get him to stop at a 7-Eleven and when I come out he's gone."

"He stole your car?"

"I don't know. Looks like it. So I call the lot and not one of the bastards will get in a car and come and get me. They think it's a big joke. So I try to get a cab and they're all backed up. So here I am slumming. But hey. I ran into you."

"Yeah. Funny."

"This is my block coming up. How the hell do you get the damned thing to stop and let you out?"

"Pull this. Hear that bell? It tells the driver you want off."

"What the hell. Hey. You want to meet for lunch someday?"

"Sure. I'm in the book."

"In the book even. And we've never run into each other."

Phil got off the bus and Sylvia watched him walk up the street. It was the north-end business district and she could see a GM dealership a block away, Phil's place of employment. Seeing him took her back to a funny time in her relationships with men. She and Phil had been close, far closer than she was to R, but they had never slept together.

"Do you like me?" Sylvia asked R in his cousin's apartment. They were snacking on crackers and some spicy cream cheese they'd found in the fridge.

"Of course I do," R said. "What a dumb question."

"I mean, do you really like me? I'm not just talking blonde hair. I know you like blondes. I want to know if you like me."

"I like you," R said.

"Do you want to know what happened to me in the cafeteria at work one day?" Sylvia asked. She was planning to tell him about the strange episode with the dishwasher.

"No," R said. "I never eat in cafeterias."

"That's irrelevant to what I'm about to tell you," Sylvia said, surprised.

"It's not irrelevant. Even talking about cafeterias puts me off my food."

Sylvia realized with shock that R was not the least bit interested in what happened to her. The next time he called her at work, she made up an excuse for being unable to meet him. It was the first time she'd done that. She didn't want to end it, but she didn't see why she had to go every single time he called.

Phil called Sylvia at home to invite her for lunch. She agreed to meet him at a downtown coffee shop. When she hung up, Eddy asked her who she'd been talking to.

"A car salesman," Sylvia said.

"Are you thinking of buying a car?" Eddy asked, with a touch of excitement in his voice.

"We're just at the talking stage," she said. "But I guess you could say I'm thinking about it."

"Great," said Eddy. "What kind of car are you looking at?"

"A Buick," Sylvia said.

Eddy looked shocked. "A Buick?"

"Yes," Sylvia said. "What's wrong with Buicks?"

"You are a really strange person," Eddy said. "I've got nothing on you for strangeness."

Afterward, Sylvia had to admit that, had Phil not backed out, she probably would have slept with him. But before they even got to dessert he'd decided he couldn't do it. She'd noticed he seemed nervous right from the time they sat down. She hadn't guessed that he was experiencing a moral dilemma.

"I was planning to try to get you into the sack," Phil said. "That's why I phoned you."

"You're kidding me," Sylvia said, feigning innocence.

"I wasn't assuming you'd want to. Don't think that. I was prepared to be turned down. But now that we're here I know I can't go through with it."

"Why not?" she asked. "Just for the sake of the discussion, I mean. Now that we're talking about it."

"I remembered that I like you. That's the problem. Because I like Fern. My wife. And I don't want to sleep with anybody else that I like. Know what I mean?"

"I guess so," Sylvia said.

"But this is how I looked at it," Phil went on. "You and I could have slept together a long time ago. If we had, it wouldn't have made any difference to Fern and me. So I thought, what would be the difference if we did it now? Boy. What you don't think up to keep from feeling guilty."

"I know what you mean," Sylvia said, although she didn't really. She didn't seem to feel guilty about R at all.

Phil laughed and showed Sylvia his shaking hands. Then he told her all about Fern and the three kids. And for some reason Sylvia found herself talking about R. She knew she should be talking about Eddy, but R just came to her lips more easily. She even led Phil to believe R was the man she was living with. Phil looked worried. He said it didn't sound to him as if Sylvia was very happy. It didn't sound as if she liked R much. Why did she stay with him? Sylvia said she didn't know.

On the rare days that Sylvia spent her lunch hour in the cafeteria, the dishwasher made her so nervous she could hardly eat. She felt as if every bit of egg salad that slid from her sandwich onto her plate would be collected by him and used as evidence against her. She always wiped her plate with a napkin before she handed it through the window and she was especially careful never to make eye contact. She clung to the belief that the dishwasher had some kind of problem with aggressive behaviour. This belief did eventually come to be shaken.

Sylvia was in line at the cafeteria counter. A young girl was working the till, a new girl who had been working for only a few days. She was slow and obviously nervous. Sylvia stared at her, trying to figure out what her particular mental disability was. The girl looked perfectly normal, except for the fact that she was wearing far too much make-up. She would even be pretty, Sylvia thought, if she didn't have ridiculous black lines under her eyes and big patches of blusher that made her look like something between a clown and a street hooker. The girl was so nervous her hands were shaking.

The woman in front of Sylvia had a bowl of soup, an apple and a glass of milk on her tray. The girl took a long time to punch the order into the till, her fingers hovering over each key before she pressed it. Finally she had a total. "That will be three dollars and forty-two cents," the girl said. The woman held out a five dollar bill. The girl took it. She was about to put the bill in the cash drawer when her hand appeared to freeze in midair. The girl was staring at the till, frozen, apparently seeing nothing. The woman waited until it became necessary to do something.

"Excuse me," she said awkwardly, "but are you all right?"

This had no effect whatsoever on the girl with the five dollar bill in her hand. People in the line-up, at least those who were too far back to see that something was wrong, were getting impatient and rude.

"What should we do?" the woman asked Sylvia. But luckily they didn't have to do anything, because the supervisor suddenly noticed the girl's stupor. She hurried over with another cafeteria worker.

"Melody," the supervisor said. "Snap out of it, Melody." Melody didn't move.

"We should get Simon," the other worker said. "She likes Simon."

"Simon," the supervisor called. "Can you come here for a minute?" She gently led Melody away from the till and took the bill from her hand. Sylvia was amazed at the gentleness. The supervisor had always seemed like such a brusque person.

"Now," she said. "Let's get this line moving again." She gave the woman in front of Sylvia her change.

"Is she going to be all right?" the woman asked.

"Oh yes, she'll be fine," the supervisor said, glancing at the frozen girl. "Sorry about the delay," she called to the line-up. "That'll be five-seventy," she said to Sylvia, then called to the kitchen, "Simon, we need you."

Simon came. He was the dishwasher. Sylvia quickly averted her eyes, but tried to watch what happened as she carried her tray to a table. Simon led the girl to the kitchen. They disappeared, and then Sylvia could see them again through the open window. Simon had his arm around the girl's shoulder and was speaking to her, touching her hair with an intimacy that made Sylvia shiver. She was puzzled. She had just seen two people touching this funny girl with incredible gentleness, and neither seemed like the kind of person who gave away grace. Simon noticed Sylvia watching them. He took himself away from the girl, who was still holding her hand above an imaginary till, and closed the window.

The people eating lunch in the cafeteria adjusted to the closure and left their trays on the tables. Sylvia jealously tried to figure out why Simon had been so cruel to her when he obviously had the capacity for kindness.

Sylvia wondered whether she should terminate her relationship with R. Whenever she tried to talk to him about anything, he cut her off. Like when she tried to tell him about the girl in the cafeteria.

"She probably *is* a street hooker," R said when Sylvia described the girl's make-up.

"I don't think so," Sylvia said. "I think she was symbolically trying to cover up her real self because— "

R interrupted. "I don't want to talk about some nutcase who

works in a cafeteria. You know what I think of cafeterias. Why did
you even bring it up?"

Sylvia didn't really know why the incident was important to
her, or why it seemed important to talk to R. She just remembered
Simon touching the girl's hair.

When she got home that night, Eddy told her he'd written a new
song. "It's called 'The Dying Swan,'" he said.

"I think that's been done before," Sylvia said.

Eddy was hurt. "Everything's been done before," he said. Then
he got defensive. "Haven't you heard of post-modernism?" he said.
"It's been done before. Jesus. What a stupid thing to say."

Sylvia went to the bedroom to change and Eddy followed her.
He watched her slip out of her work clothes.

"The trouble with you is you don't take me seriously," he said.
"You don't see my music as a job equal to yours."

"I don't spend my days all doped up," Sylvia said.

"Oh don't you," Eddy said. "Don't you. It seems to me your life
is one big anaesthetic."

"What's that supposed to mean?" she said, getting down on
her hands and knees to look for a pair of shoes under the bed. She
was thinking, he doesn't know about R. Then Eddy said, "Your
noon hours in particular," and she realized he did know about R.

She was looking for a pair of red suede shoes that looked
especially nice with jeans and she couldn't find them. She kept
pulling shoes out from under the bed and none of them matched.
Eddy stood in the doorway, enveloped in smoke, watching her. She
finally sat back on the floor, surrounded by shoes, none of them
the ones she was looking for.

"I hate the way we live," she said to him.

"What do you mean?" he asked quietly. She knew he was
giving her an opening. She couldn't take it.

"Most people keep their shoes in a closet," she said. "On a rack
or at least lined up in pairs."

"Don't blame me," Eddy said. "They're all yours."

He was right. Eddy had one pair of shoes, cowboy boots, and he
was wearing them.

"Nonetheless," she said. "I hate the way we live."

Eddy left the room and Sylvia put her head down on the bed

and cried for a while. She could hear Eddy's guitar in the living room, playing what she supposed was "The Dying Swan." He was a good guitar player. Everybody said so.

When she was done crying she decided she'd call up Phil and ask him to sell her a car. Maybe Eddy had something with that talk about the country drives. She pictured the two of them heading out in a Buick every Sunday instead of hanging around an apartment full of smoke and clutter.

Devil's Hill

STEVIE had always wanted a black leather motorcycle jacket so she bought one with her first pay cheque after she started working full-time at the jewellery store. She didn't wear it much at first because she felt self-conscious. She left it hanging on the back of a kitchen chair where she could admire it, and sometimes she'd wear it over her nightgown instead of a housecoat. Eventually, she started wearing the jacket outside and now she doesn't even think about it. Joel's brother Derrick had one almost the same. Now Joel has it.

Stevie thinks she loves Joel, but she doesn't know for sure and she doesn't want to know. She might be leaving in the fall, leaving Devil's Hill for good, and loving Joel would be a complication. Joel says that he loves her, but she thinks things are confusing for him right now because of his brother being dead. She doesn't want to be responsible for making things more confusing so she hasn't told him she's considering going away to school, that she's thinking the risk might be worth it. She doesn't want to lose him, but after all, it's her life she's talking about.

It's the middle of a hot summer and Stevie watches for Joel from the Shell station, where she now has a job pumping gas. He should be at work on the paving crew but he isn't there and she doesn't know where he is. It's not like him to miss work.

"Hey Stevie, where's your boyfriend?"

It's Dave. He's standing behind her, almost touching her, and she'd like to swat at him like you would a fly buzzing around your head.

"You don't know where he is, do you," says Dave.

"It's none of your business whether I know or not," Stevie says.

A half-ton pulls up to one of the full-service pumps, the first vehicle in ages, and Dave says, "You get it. I have to see a man about a horse." He heads for the washroom, but then the truck pulls over to the self-serve and Dave comes back. "Guess I was wrong," Dave says. "I don't have to go after all."

"Maybe you should go for a check-up," Stevie says. "There's something wrong with your water works. Maybe it's going to fall off."

"Break your heart if it did," Dave says.

"You wish," says Stevie.

The Shell is on the edge of town, right where they're building the new divided highway. It's usually a busy tourist stop, but this summer the road construction has really cut into business. Fifteen or twenty minutes often goes by without a car pulling in for gas because nobody can figure out how to get to the service road from the detour. Stevie keeps expecting to be laid off, but Jake Jr. doesn't seem to care that he's got too many people working for him. There are six of them altogether, and usually Stevie works shift with a guy named Brendan, who was in her class at school. Sometimes, like today, she's on with Dave. She hates Dave. When the truck driver has finished filling up, Dave is there like a shot to take his money.

Stevie lasted at Fiddlers Jewellery downtown for not quite a year. Mr. Fiddler drove her crazy. All he could talk about was the new mall and how it was ruining his life, and he was always on her case about selling more watches and diamonds. He wanted her to put pressure on people, which she didn't want to do, and the final straw came when he called her into the back of the store one day and told her not to wear the motorcycle jacket to work anymore. She said she didn't wear her jacket in the store so she didn't think it was any of his business, and he said he was concerned about what people would think when they saw her on the street.

"Everybody in Devil's Hill knows you're my employee," Mr. Fiddler said.

"Not everybody," she said. "It's not *that* small a town."

"You know what I mean," he said. And then he said, "I could

fire you in a minute. I hardly need the help anyway. The new mall's taking all my business."

"Maybe you should just move up to the mall," she said.

"My father would roll over in his grave," he said. "He built this store, even helped lay the bricks. If he were alive, he would certainly fire you for coming to work in that jacket."

"It's just a leather jacket," she said.

"But what does a jacket like that mean?" he said. "How can people be expected to trust someone who wears a jacket with all those zippers?"

"That is so dumb," she said, and then she quit. It was just a minimum wage job anyway because she didn't ever sell enough to get paid commission.

The jacket is right now hanging in Jake Jr.'s office in the service station and Stevie thinks how stupid it was to bring it with her on such a hot day. Her arm was covered with sweat from carrying it and now she has a prickly rash.

The paving crew is just a hundred yards away from the Shell, and if Joel were there Stevie would be able to see him. She watches through the heat rising from the thick black surface. She would hate to work on a paving crew, hour after hour of sweat and stinking hot asphalt. She at least can go to the washroom and run cold tap water whenever she wants, splash it on her face and down the back of her neck. Once she and Brendan had a water fight with the bug water buckets, and even though the water was lukewarm and disgusting it cooled them off and killed the time until their shift was up.

If business were better they wouldn't have to worry about killing time, but Jake Sr., the station owner, is in the hospital so he can't try to make the Department of Highways build a less complicated temporary approach. His son Jake Jr. is supposed to be running the place, but he's busy with his own life and he isn't around much at all, except to open in the morning and lock up at midnight. He knows things aren't going well and he doesn't seem to care. Stevie wishes he'd come around more often so he'd see what Dave is up to and fire him. She's seen Dave help himself to money from the till, a few bucks here, a few there. Dave knows she knows and once he tried to entice her to join in, as though it were just a little game. Stevie told him she wasn't interested and now he won't leave her alone. She hates working the same shift as him. He follows her around, breathing down her neck, and he usually says something disgusting when he catches her watching Joel.

Joel is a raker on the paving crew and his job is to follow the paver and rake the seam where two beds of asphalt overlap. The asphalt plant shuts down at six o'clock every day and Joel and the paver operator work until they're out of asphalt. After the paver operator shuts down, Joel bevels the end of the asphalt bed and lays a strip of tar paper over it so it will stay soft for the next load in the morning. Except for Saturdays, he has no fixed quitting time, just whenever he's finished, unless it's raining so hard it cools the asphalt down and they have to quit early, but that's happened only twice this summer. Usually it's hot and Joel's out there doing his same hot job. Not today though. Someone else is raking behind the paver. Stevie can't imagine where Joel could be. She supposes he could be sick, but she saw him last night and he was fine then.

Stevie and Joel don't live together. It's never come up and Stevie assumes it won't, not for a while anyway, because Joel is worried about leaving his mother to live alone on the farm. Stevie lives in the Derksons' basement suite in town. She was best friends with Shannon Derkson in highschool and she moved into the Derksons' suite when she had a big fight with her mother toward the end of grade twelve. Stevie had been skipping classes to hang out with her boyfriend, not Joel, who had dropped out of school. Although the Derksons' was supposed to be a temporary arrangement, Stevie liked living on her own so she got a part-time job at a car wash that earned her just enough money to pay the rent. Even after she broke up with the boyfriend and got straightened out at school, she continued to live at the Derksons'.

The suite isn't so great now because Mrs. Derkson doesn't like Joel staying overnight, which he does sometimes. Mrs. Derkson doesn't seem to like Stevie anymore either, now that Shannon has moved away from home. She takes every opportunity to be rude, except when Stevie gives her the rent cheque, she's polite enough then. Joel thinks Stevie should get another place but she doesn't want to because Mrs. Derkson's is cheap and she can save money even though she's earning only minimum wage. She could move back home, but she suspects that wouldn't work out, not with

Joel. Stevie and her mother get along fine now and Stevie wants things to stay that way.

Joel doesn't know Stevie is thinking about going away to school, that she's already applied, just in case. He knows she'll probably be laid off at the Shell when the tourist season is over, and he thinks he can get her on as the bookkeeper at Gary's Esso, where he works in the winter. Gary's wife used to do the books but now he does them himself and he's told Joel that he's going to have to hire someone if Lynn doesn't decide she's ready to face the world again pretty soon. Stevie hasn't ever done anything like books, but Joel knows she was good at math in school and he tells her she can learn to do it, no problem. Stevie is pretty sure that's true, but bookkeeping is not something she particularly wants to learn.

Stevie watches the paving crew and thinks how strange it is that it worked out this way with their jobs, that most days she knows exactly where Joel is every minute. She wonders if he ever watches her. He doesn't seem to. She came right out and asked him once and he said he didn't have time to watch her, he was too busy working. He teased her, saying she was lucky to have the kind of job where she could stand around and gawk all day, and then he said she probably couldn't keep her eyes off his body when he was out there on the highway, using his muscles and sweating.

"Don't you ever watch me just to see what I'm doing?" Stevie asked.

"No," Joel said.

"Why not?" she asked. "Don't you want to know about me, what I'm like when I'm not with you?" She was thinking about the time she had the water fight with Brendan and whether Joel had seen and what he might have thought about it.

"I don't want anyone to see me staring at you," Joel said. "It's too personal."

Stevie knows what Joel is like, the way he keeps things to himself. Still, she doesn't know why he isn't more curious. She's curious about men and what they think about their lives, and she keeps asking him questions about his job and what it's like to work that hard. He says he doesn't know why she has to ask because it's common sense and she should know just by looking. She doesn't know, though. There's a lot she doesn't know and it all has to do with how he is inside. She thinks about him wearing Derrick's jacket. She'd like to ask him how he feels when he's wearing it, but she won't. She knows that would be going too far.

Joel does tell her stories about the men who work on the crew. She's particularly interested in the checker, a university student named Roland, who works for the Department of Highways and not for the contractor like the rest of them. Roland is a tall skinny kid who wears a hard-hat with Spike written on it, no one knows why. Maybe it's his nickname, or maybe the hard-hat was someone else's, some other checker from another summer. His job is to keep track of things, like how many loads of asphalt get delivered, and every once in a while he sticks a thermometer in the asphalt to check the temperature. He keeps a logbook and nobody talks to him much. Stevie decides he must be lonely, but when she says this to Joel he tells her to save her sympathy for the wobbly driver, who is old and has worked on highway crews most of his life.

"How'd you like to have that to look back on for a lifetime?" Joel says to her.

"Not me," she says.

"Me neither," he says.

Joel claims that the highway job is temporary, one that earns him double the money he could earn working at Gary's Esso. He imagines that he will own a business like that someday, maybe even the Esso. Gary did talk to him and Derrick once about the possibility of their taking over from him, although it was understood he was talking several years down the road.

Joel's been working off and on at Gary's for five years, since he was fifteen. Derrick started there first and then he got Joel on. Joel is like a son to Gary, who doesn't have children of his own, and Stevie thinks that maybe Joel *will* end up with the garage. She wouldn't be surprised. She wonders how Joel feels when he imagines himself running it alone, without Derrick, because that's how it would have to be, no matter what they talked about before.

A few weeks after Stevie and Joel started going together, there was a fight in the parking lot at a country dance and Derrick was stabbed by Amos Quinn. The knife went into the lower right side of his abdomen, just a few inches below the bottom of his jacket, and hit an artery. He died in the back seat of his friend Jeff's car, with no-one knowing how badly hurt he really was because it had been just a little jackknife and there wasn't much blood. They were on their way to the hospital in town to get Derrick checked out, talking about the fight and how they'd get that son-of-a-bitch Quinn for pulling a knife. Derrick was lying down in the back seat because he didn't feel too good, and at some point Jeff noticed that Derrick wasn't talking anymore. Jeff drove the rest of the way to town at a hundred and twenty, but it was too late. Derrick was gone by the time they got to the hospital.

Joel and Stevie had been at the dance, but they weren't there when the fight broke out. They were in Stevie's basement suite in town. At midnight Mrs. Derkson started pounding on the floor above the bedroom to let them know she knew Joel was there and she didn't like it. Stevie didn't want Joel to leave and said if they just ignored her she'd give up and get used to Joel being there, but Joel said he had to go anyway because he had heard rumours earlier that Amos Quinn was going to be looking for Derrick and he wanted to see if anything had come of it. He went back to the dance, and that's when he heard there'd been a fight and Derrick had been stabbed.

Joel didn't bother going after Jeff and Derrick to the hospital because everyone said it was nothing. Instead, he and a carload of his and Derrick's friends drove around the country looking for Amos Quinn. When they couldn't find him, Joel went home. The police were already there with his mother and that's how he found out Derrick was dead. One of Joel's friends phoned Stevie the next morning to tell her and she didn't know what to do. She'd never been close to a death before. She waited by the phone for Joel to call, and when he didn't she grew afraid that maybe he would never call her again because his life would be so changed.

He showed up at the door three days later wearing a suit and shiny black shoes. He usually wore jeans and T-shirts, and he didn't look like the same person. He said he'd just been to prayers at the funeral home, without saying who the prayers were for. They sat on Stevie's couch and talked for a bit, but not about Derrick or the fight. Then Joel said he wanted to go dancing. Stevie was wearing an old grey sweatsuit and she wanted to change but Joel wouldn't let her. He said there wasn't time, he wanted to go dancing right away or he'd lose the urge. They went out to a bar

that had a house band and they danced until the bar closed. Stevie
felt odd dancing with Joel in his suit, partly because of how she was
dressed, but also because she'd never seen him in a suit before.

When Joel dropped Stevie off at home, he didn't go in with her.
He kissed her good night and then he casually said that he wanted
her to go to the funeral with him. Stevie talked to her mother on
the phone the next day and her mother advised her that it wouldn't
be right to go and sit with the family because she and Joel hadn't
been going out very long. Maybe Joel's mother told Joel the same
thing, because he didn't call for her. Stevie thought she should go
to the funeral anyway. She had met Derrick a few times and she
had, after all, been at the dance.

She sat in the balcony of the church and studied the people
below her. It was a big church and the funeral crowd didn't half fill
it. There were several empty rows separating the family in the
front pew from the rest of the mourners, and the empty rows made
Joel's family look small and lonely, like they were expecting more
relatives who didn't come. Stevie was the only one in the balcony,
except for a woman with a baby and two small children. The
woman left early in the service when the baby began to fuss.

Stevie picked out Gary's head from the back and was surprised
to see that his wife was with him. She'd never met Lynn, but she
knew that she didn't go out anymore, although she didn't know
why. Nobody seemed to, not even Gary. Lynn was dressed completely in black. Her red hair was mostly covered with a black
scarf, and when she turned her head Stevie saw that she was
wearing black sunglasses. She looked like a French movie star.
Gary kept his arm around her shoulders the whole time.

Stevie watched Joel too, and wondered what it would be like to
lose your brother, someone you'd grown up with. She thought
perhaps you'd feel that pieces of yourself were lost because when
you're close to someone, you overlap. But at the end of the service
Joel followed Derrick's body from the church, walking tall and
straight, displaying no missing pieces. He walked behind his
mother and his divorced sister, Abbey, who held her mother's arm
tightly. His other sister, Anne, walked behind him, and there was
a terrible moment when Anne broke down and Joel turned and
lifted her into the arms of her husband, who carried her from the
church as though she were a small child. Stevie left the balcony

quickly then, through the back door and the Sunday school rooms. She knew that she was not yet a part of Joel's life, not really, even though she felt close to him and often wanted to lose herself inside of him.

She went back to her suite and waited for him. A week went by and he still hadn't called. She was frantic, but when he finally came they went to a movie and then they went back to her place and made love. Mrs. Derkson pounded on the floor above them and Joel frightened Stevie, first with his anger and then with his intensity. He bit her on the shoulder and left a small bruise that lasted for days. She looked at the bruise often in the mirror, wondering what it meant and where it had come from. She imagined the bruise inside of Joel, trapped in a small dark place, fighting its way out.

It's seven o'clock and Stevie's shift ends at midnight. She watches a truck back up to the paver with what is probably the last load of asphalt for the day. The driver puts the truck in neutral and lets the paver push it along as the asphalt gets dumped into a kind of hopper on the front of the paver. Stevie knows how this works because Joel explained it one day when she asked.

Usually when she works late Joel picks her up and drives her home. She wonders if he'll come tonight. She decides to phone his mother's and find out if he's sick, but when she does there's no answer. He can't be sick then, and she's relieved because they have plans for tomorrow.

Tomorrow is Saturday. Joel gets off at three on Saturdays, his only day with a regular quitting time, and Stevie has an early shift. They're supposed to go to Lynn and Gary's. Out of the blue one night last week Gary said, "Lynn wants to know if you two can come for supper on Saturday night." They were at the Esso on the south side, drinking beer in Gary's office.

"So what do you say?" Gary asked again. "Saturday night? Say, five-thirty, six o'clock?"

"Sure," Joel said. "Five-thirty. Is that okay with you, Stevie?"

"Yeah," Stevie said. "That's great."

"Lynn's been going through the recipe books and making lists a mile long," Gary said. "Whatever she settles on, it's bound to be good."

Joel looked like he was about to ask something, then he thought better of it. Gary knew, though, and he said, "She seems to be getting back to her old self."

"That's good," Joel said quickly. "That's good, Gary. I hope you're right."

Stevie was glad that Joel had accepted the supper invitation. Although she was nervous about meeting Lynn, she looked forward to it. She remembered Lynn looking mysterious at Derrick's funeral, and she was interested in the fact that Lynn and Gary had got married so young. At least Lynn was young, she was only seventeen. Gary was older by ten years and he already owned the Esso. Lynn had been planning to go to university somewhere and study art, but then she fell in love with Gary and changed her mind. They got married when she was in grade twelve. She was taking a class called Family Life where the teacher was afraid to talk about sex and birth control, and when Lynn started asking questions that were too sophisticated she was excused from the class for the rest of the term. The principal said she was already married and there was no point. She got a B without even going to the class. Lynn had told Joel and Derrick that story one day when she was still hanging around the garage.

According to Joel, Lynn used to drop by the Esso quite a bit to pick up receipts and other things she needed for the books. She'd stay and work the till or maybe just hang around and shoot the breeze. Sometimes, if Gary was too busy at the garage to get home for lunch or supper, Joel and Derrick would pick Lynn up and take her to the A & W for burgers. She pulled beer for them before they were old enough to buy their own. Once she gave them each haircuts on a stool in her kitchen. Derrick went first. He had a ponytail then and he was sick of it and wanted Lynn to cut it off. Joel said that Lynn laughed so hard the whole time she was cutting they were afraid of what Derrick was going to look like, afraid he was going to have to get his head shaved. She did a good job, though, and afterward she told them she'd taken a hairdressing course by correspondence, which got them laughing again because how could you cut hair by correspondence? She said she'd done a lot of practising on Gary, but then his hair started to fall out and it became a joke that Lynn had caused him to go bald.

The supper invitation was a surprise to Stevie. Although

no-one ever said that Lynn had an actual mental illness, that was certainly the impression Stevie had because of Lynn's refusal to go out or see people anymore. Stevie asked Joel once what had happened to her, why things changed, but he didn't know. He said Gary didn't seem to know either. At first she wouldn't go out in the evenings, to a movie or for Chinese food. Then she stopped dropping by the garage, and she quit going for groceries and taking the dry cleaning downtown, even going to the post office for stamps. Eventually, Gary was doing everything that had to be done outside of the house. Either Gary did it, or Lynn found a way to get whatever she needed over the telephone. Stevie asked Joel if he thought there was something wrong with their marriage, like did Lynn want a divorce maybe, but Joel said you could tell they were still in love by the way Gary talked about her.

It's clear to Stevie that Joel misses Lynn. The only time he'd seen her in the last year was at the graveside after Derrick's funeral and he hadn't had a chance to talk to her. When Joel asked Gary later how he'd got Lynn out to the funeral, Gary said it was her idea.

"Maybe she's coming out of it," Joel said to Stevie when he dropped her off at home after they finished their beers with Gary. "Whatever was the matter with her."

"I hope so," Stevie said.

"I don't know much about it, what goes on in a person's head," Joel said. "Usually I don't want to know. I've thought about Lynn though. I feel bad about what's happened to her. And Gary too."

"I think most people kind of go day to day," Stevie said.

"What do you mean?" Joel asked.

"It's just that day to day might not have been good enough for Lynn," Stevie said. "Of course I don't know. I've never met her."

"I don't have a clue why people are the way they are," Joel said. "It's all beyond me."

"Think about the paving crew," Stevie said. "If that were day to day for you ... Well. You know what I mean."

"I'd end up the old guy driving the wobbly," Joel said.

"I'm not sure what this has to do with Lynn," Stevie said, wondering if she should tell Joel it wasn't Lynn she was thinking about now, it was herself. "I guess I kind of got sidetracked in my thinking."

"Maybe all you mean is, Lynn's unhappy," Joel said.

"Yes," Stevie said. "That is what I meant." Then she said, "I think I love you, Joel." She felt funny saying it. They were still sitting in Joel's car out in front of her place. She couldn't look at him.

"You think?" he asked. "Is that all?"

"It's quite a lot," Stevie said. "You say you love me, but I don't know if you do."

"Do you want me to cut off my ear?" Joel asked.

"That's not what I meant," Stevie said. "I just meant, thinking might be all there is. You might not ever know for sure. We might as well be honest about it."

Joel looked kind of hurt, but he didn't look angry and Stevie was glad she had said it.

Stevie watches as the packer operator shuts down and the raker, the one that isn't Joel, finishes raking the seam and then lays tar paper over the end of the asphalt bed. Roland the checker hovers around for a bit and then he gets in a Department of Highways truck. Stevie imagines him going back to a little room somewhere and heating up a frozen meat pie for supper. She imagines how glad he will be when the summer is over and he can go back to university and get on with being an engineer or whatever it is he wants to be.

Dave is leaning against one of the pumps drinking a Coke as Stevie watches Roland drive away and tries to figure out where Joel could be.

"Your boyfriend hasn't been at work all day, has he," Dave says.

"I don't know where he is every second," she says. "I'm not his mother."

"He's probably at home sleeping," Dave says. "I'm sure that was him I saw last night. He was with this great looking babe. Blonde. Big tits. Maybe you know her."

"Fuck off, Dave," she says. Then before she can stop herself, because he's been bothering her all day, she says, "Fuck off or I'll tell Jake Jr. about the money."

Dave has her up against the pump before she can even think about getting out of his way. He pins her with one hand and with the other he grabs her breast and squeezes, not hard, just hard enough to let her know he could really hurt her if he wanted to. She pushes against him but he's strong and he holds her there and squeezes, just hard enough, and then he lets her go and takes a hard kick at his Coke can, which is lying where he dropped it on the pavement.

Stevie runs for the washroom on the east side of the building, the women's side. She fishes in her pocket for the key, but sees she doesn't need it because someone has left the door wide open again. She slams it closed after herself and it locks automatically. Son-of-a-bitch, she says over and over again, kicking the locked door, fucking stinking son-of-a-bitch. She imagines drenching Dave with gasoline from one of the pumps and then throwing a match on him. She watches until he's nothing but a pile of blackened bones, then she kicks hard and scatters his bones across the pavement.

She goes to the sink and turns on the tap. She splashes water on her face and down the back of her neck, not waiting for the water to run cold. As she looks at herself in the mirror, warm water dripping off her face and hair, she thinks that everything has changed. She is afraid of Dave now, and she realizes that fear makes her feel smaller.

When she hears a car pull up to the pumps and honk she comes out. She watches from the corner of the building as Dave fills the tank and washes the windshield. She can hear him talking to the driver about the weather and the highway construction. The driver of the car pays Dave cash and pulls out onto the service road. Stevie stays well back, close to the washroom door, but Dave knows she's there. He looks right at her, waves a ten-dollar bill in the air, and then pockets it. He says, "I'm leaving early. Tell Jake I got food poisoning from my tuna sandwich." He goes inside and rings in the sale and when he comes out he says to Stevie, "I'm off tomorrow, but I see we work the same shift next week. I'm looking forward to it." He gets in his car and drives away. Stevie doesn't know what she would have done if he hadn't.

It's after midnight before Jake Jr. arrives to lock up. There's no sign of Joel. Stevie gets her jacket and says good night to Jake without mentioning that Dave left early. She's almost to the door when Jake says, "Would you stay for just a minute, Stevie. There's something I want to talk to you about."

As Jake counts cash, she hangs around wondering what's up, hoping it doesn't have anything to do with the till. When he's done he says, "It's been short every day this week and I'm getting sick and tired of it." He looks at Stevie. "Do you know anything about this? You've been on every day. It doesn't look good for you."

She tries not to let show that she knows anything about the money. She tries to look shocked.

"What do you mean?" she asks.

Jake looks at her, then says, "Okay. I know it's not you. But someone who works here is as crooked as the day is long."

"It's not me," she says.

Jake puts the money he's counted in a canvas bag and shuts the till drawer.

"It must be Dave," he says. He looks tired. "I don't want this job," he says. "I've got a job already. I don't want to have anything to do with this place."

There is an awkward moment in which neither of them knows what to say, then Stevie asks, "How is your father?"

"Not good," Jake says. "He'll live, but that's about it."

"I'm sorry," she says. She wants to say more, but she doesn't know what. "I don't mean to pry," she says, "but I heard he's paralysed."

"I'm afraid that's true," he says. "From the chest down."

"Maybe he'll recover," she says. "You read about miraculous recoveries all the time."

"You might as well go home," he says. "I don't know why I asked you to stay. I didn't think it was you."

Stevie turns to go.

"Don't say anything about this to Dave," Jake says. "I want to catch the son-of-a-bitch." He adds, "If you wait a minute I'll give you a ride. I see your boyfriend isn't here."

"No thanks," Stevie says. Then she changes her mind because Dave might be waiting for her somewhere.

All the way to Mrs. Derkson's, Jake Jr. says nothing and Stevie thinks about the money and Dave. She wants to bust him, tell Jake everything, but she's afraid to. She decides she'll do nothing and let him get caught, but then she thinks maybe that wouldn't be a good idea either, Dave might think she told. She could warn Dave that Jake suspects him, but then he'll quit taking the money and Jake will know she said something. Or maybe Jake will think it was her taking the money after all, if it stops now. Why should he believe her anyway? She doesn't know why he believed her tonight, when she thinks about it. All the way home, she doesn't know what to do. She wants Dave to get caught, but she's afraid of him. She can still feel his hand on her breast, squeezing, can see his face warning her that he is not afraid.

When they pull up in front of Mrs. Derkson's, Stevie starts to get out without her leather jacket. Jake Jr. hands it to her.

"You're a nice girl, Stevie," he says. "I don't know why you wear a jacket like this."

"It's just a jacket," she says. "It doesn't mean I'm in a motorcycle gang or anything."

"That boy's brother was stabbed," he says. "You'd better watch yourself."

"I don't mean to be disrespectful," she says, "but was it your father's fault he was in that terrible accident?"

"It was his misfortune," Jake says.

Stevie gets out of the car. "Thanks for the ride," she says. "I hope you figure out who's stealing from you."

When she gets downstairs, the local paper is lying on the floor in front of her door. A headline in the top right-hand corner catches her eye. The headline says, "Two year sentence for Quinn." She reads the article and finds out that this morning Amos Quinn was sentenced after pleading guilty to a lesser charge of manslaughter. Two years less a day. Stevie now knows why Joel was not at work.

Joel phones early on Saturday morning to tell Stevie he'll pick her up later in the afternoon. He doesn't say anything about the sentence, so she doesn't ask. All morning she thinks about it, and she thinks about Dave and what to do. She decides she will tell Joel about the money and what Dave did to her, and then she decides she won't because Joel has enough to do hating Amos Quinn.

Joel picks her up at about four o'clock and they drive out of town instead of to Lynn and Gary's. Derrick's leather jacket is on the seat between them. Stevie hasn't brought her own jacket because it's another hot day, even hotter than the day before. She looks at Derrick's jacket and thinks about him wearing it the night he died. She thinks, if it had just been a few inches longer it would have stopped the knife. Then she wonders if that's even true, or if it's just one of those things you say, trying to believe such a terrible thing could have been prevented.

She decides they must be going to Joel's place.

"Are we going to pick up your mother?" she asks, thinking that perhaps his mother has been invited to Lynn and Gary's too.

"No," Joel says. "She's gone to Anne's. I drove her there just before I picked you up."

He turns off onto a back road and Stevie realizes they're going to the country hall where the fight was. Joel has not mentioned Amos Quinn or the sentence.

When they get to the hall he turns the motor off and they sit in the car. Nothing looks out of the ordinary. It's a quiet little country hall with red asphalt shingles and a dirt parking lot. There are pots of red geraniums on both sides of the door. A grey-haired woman carrying a water bucket comes around the corner from behind the hall. She stops and looks at Joel and Stevie, then she waters the geraniums.

"That's Mrs. Craig," Joel says. "She lives just up the road. She thinks she owns the damn place."

Stevie hadn't noticed the flowers the night of the dance, but maybe it had been too early in the spring. And it had been dark, and there were a lot of people standing around the step. She'd felt like a bit of a celebrity that night because she was Joel's new girlfriend, a town girl, and everyone wanted to get a look at her.

Joel gets out of the car and walks past Mrs. Craig to a spot just west of the hall. Stevie doesn't know if she is to follow him, but she does. She says hello to Mrs. Craig on her way by and Mrs. Craig doesn't answer, just watches her suspiciously.

Joel stops and stares at the ground. "Right about here," he says, perhaps to Stevie. He takes a few deep breaths, then returns to the car. Stevie follows. As they are getting in the car, Mrs. Craig says, "We don't need trouble here."

Joel says under his breath, "Shut up, you old cow."

Mrs. Craig says, "I hope you heard me. We've seen nothing but police around here all summer and it gives the wrong impression."

"Mind your own damn business," Joel says to Mrs. Craig and slams the car door.

They drive very slowly toward town. Joel stares hard at the road as though he's taking in every detail, every pebble, every blade of grass that has inched from the ditch and broken through the packed gravel bed. He's so intent it seems he's hardly aware that Stevie is in the car. She studies his face, looks for clues, but she can't tell what's going through his head. It's worse than the first night he came to see her after Derrick died. He'd been more like himself then, even in the suit.

He slows the car to barely a crawl. They cross a little bridge, round a curve, and stop.

"Right about here," Joel says after a minute. "Right about here." Stevie understands. Joel puts on the leather jacket even though it's much too hot. He gets out of the car and walks around it a couple of times, then he stands staring down at the road. Stevie gets out and goes to him.

"Do you want me to leave for a bit?" she asks. "If you want to be alone, I could go for a little walk. Back along the creek. I wouldn't mind."

Joel shakes his head. A truck passes them and Stevie watches the cloud of dust rise and follow it. She can smell the dust, and the sweet clover in the ditch.

"We decided we wouldn't say much," Joel says. He takes off the jacket again and holds it as though he doesn't know what to do with it. Stevie takes it from him. "About the trial," Joel says. "Mother didn't want to talk about it, so we just decided we wouldn't." He breathes deeply, but he is in control of his voice. "She wanted to go to the courthouse, so I took her. She was counting on them to make him pay for Derrick's life."

Stevie reaches out to take his hand, but he pulls it away.

"What do you think a life is worth?" he asks, looking down the road into the distance now.

She shakes her head. "I don't know," she says.

"Ten years? Twenty?"

Stevie knows she should be on his side, and in a way she is. She believes Amos Quinn should pay no matter what the circumstances, because a life is a life and there's nothing more than that. But she is not certain. Joel is certain, but she is not and she can't wish Amos Quinn a life sentence.

"I don't know, Joel," she says. "I don't know how these things work."

"No," he says, looking at her now. "Don't say something easy like that. You know what I mean. How many years? Ten? Twenty? A lifetime?"

She tries to phrase her thoughts gently. "I can wish him years of misery. Maybe even a lifetime of it. But I imagine that's already in the cards."

"That means nothing to me," he says. Another car passes them and this time the driver honks.

"Fuck you," Joel shouts, then he looks at Stevie again. "My mother was counting on them to say Derrick's life was worth something. What she found out yesterday was that Derrick was worth two years. Not even two years. Two years less a day. Jesus." He looks away from her. "Right about here," he says one more time, and then he gets back in the car.

Stevie gets in on the passenger side. She folds Derrick's jacket carefully and lays it on the seat between them.

"I don't know what to say, Joel," she says. "I want to say the right thing, but I don't know what that is."

He starts the car and jams the gas pedal to the floor. The car fishtails and gravel flies from under the tires. Stevie screams. Joel drives into town at breakneck speed.

They pull into the driveway of Gary and Lynn's big ranch-style house on the edge of town and walk around to the back yard, which slopes gently down toward the creek. Across the creek the golf course stretches to the west. Devil's Hill, the landmark after which the town was named, rises beyond the golf course and Stevie can see golfers dotted all over the greens and the dry, yellow fairways.

Gary is waiting for them on the long wooden deck, where a picnic table is set with a white linen tablecloth and china and silverware. A bottle of wine is open with two wine glasses beside it. Gary pulls two cans of beer from a cooler on the deck for himself and Joel, then pours wine into one of the glasses. Stevie looks through the patio doors. Lynn is nowhere in sight. A hot wind is blowing and it lifts the edges of the white tablecloth.

"Sit down," Gary says, motioning toward plastic chairs with blue covers. "Mosquitoes bothering you yet? I'll light a coil if they are."

Stevie shakes her head. She and Joel sit down and Gary hands her the wine when he sees she hasn't picked it up herself.

"Being polite, eh," he says. "No need for that here."

Stevie takes the glass. She looks out over the creek and the golf course, and she watches Joel as he drains his beer too quickly. He steps on the can and flattens it, then tosses it into a plastic laundry basket half full of empties, and helps himself to another.

"Where's Lynn?" he asks.

"She'll be here in a minute," Gary says. "She's fixing her hair or her make-up or some other damn thing."

Gary goes inside and comes back carrying a plate of broiled shrimp wrapped in bacon and speared with coloured plastic toothpicks.

"Lynn loves to cook," he says, passing the hors d'oeuvres. "She's been cooking all afternoon, getting ready for this. I've had to drive up to the mall three times for different things. Cream cheese once. Then some kind of spice with a name I can't say. I had to write it down on a piece of paper. And then she wanted maraschino cherries, I don't know what for."

"I don't mind cooking," Stevie says. "I could help, if Lynn needs it."

"Far as I know, everything's taken care of," Gary says. "You could go and have a look in the kitchen if you want, see if you see something that needs doing."

Stevie takes her wine and finds her way to the kitchen.

"You ever get the feeling you're target practice?" she hears Joel ask Gary. At first she doesn't know what he means, but then she realizes he's talking about golfers.

In the kitchen the radio is on and Stevie hears the announcer issue a weather watch with a chance of heavy rain. Stevie hollers at Gary and Joel, and Gary checks out the sky and says it's all clear.

Lynn's kitchen is a big modern one. She has an island with a bright green ceramic tile counter top, and a fridge with an ice water maker in the door. The supper seems to be under control as far as Stevie can see. There's a green salad on the counter in a big wooden bowl, and the dressing is in a glass beside it. Four steaks are marinating on a platter and a potato salad with radishes sliced to look like roses is waiting under plastic wrap. Stevie looks under a white napkin and finds several kinds of freshly made buns lined up neatly in a basket. A carrot cake with cream cheese icing is also covered with plastic wrap, more of the coloured toothpicks inserted in the cake to keep the wrap from sticking. The only thing she sees that she might do is toss the salad, and she doesn't want to do that in case Lynn is fussy about waiting until just before it's time to eat.

She decides to join Joel and Gary, and as she steps through the patio doors she hears Gary say, "You'll do nothing of the kind. I mean it, Joel. You get that out of your head altogether."

They might have been father and son arguing in an ordinary kind of way, but then Joel says, "The son-of-a-bitch has to pay." His voice is tight and angry.

"He'll pay," Gary says. "Don't you worry. He'll pay in ways you can't even imagine."

"A fucking deuce," Joel says. "What the hell kind of payment is that?"

"Leave it lie, Joel," Gary says. "My advice to you is, leave it lie."

Stevie realizes that Joel is talking about revenge. He's leaning on the deck railing, his white T-shirt catching the sun, talking about making Amos Quinn pay in desperate ways.

"One thing is sure," Joel says. "Two years is a short enough time that nobody is going to forget. If they aren't going to make him pay, somebody else will. And afterwards, you can testify in a courtroom that I said that. I won't deny I said it."

Stevie doesn't know if Joel's seen her in the doorway or not. He hasn't looked at her.

"I'm not saying you're wrong," Gary says. "I don't think you are. All I'm saying is, there's no point disappearing down the road following the ass-end of something. There's no point to that."

"He'll pay," Joel says.

"That's enough, Joel," Gary says. "Do you hear me?"

"I hear you," Joel says. "Just like I hear everyone else."

He sits down in a deck chair and he still doesn't look at Stevie, and now it's obvious that he's trying not to. He stares down at his boots. Stevie doesn't believe he is angry with her. She believes he doesn't want her to see this, but there's nothing he can do to stop, just like there was nothing he could do to stop himself from driving too fast on the way into town.

"Any sign of a storm?" she asks, trying to gain control of the evening the way she knows Gary is trying.

"Not yet," Gary says. "I think you must have been listening to reruns. The sky's as blue as a robin's egg. How's your wine? Ready for another?"

She nods and Gary fills her glass.

"How about you, Joel?" Gary asks. "You ready for another cold one?"

Joel doesn't answer.

"I can tell you one thing," Gary says. "I may take up golfing one of these years, but I'll never own one of those motorized golf carts. Look at those assholes. What do you think, Joel? Want to own one of those machines?"

Joel tips his beer upside down and lets it pour from the can onto the toes of his boots. Then he pitches the can over the side of the deck onto Gary's lawn.

"In the winter," Gary says, "those same assholes rip around here on their snowmobiles. I wouldn't own a snowmobile if I won it as a door prize."

"My uncle has horses," Stevie says, knowing the conversation is leaning in a ridiculous direction for Joel's sake. "North of town. Quite a ways north, really. You wouldn't know him, I don't imagine."

Gary looks puzzled.

"He says in the winter people from town run his horses with their snowmobiles. Just for fun."

"You're kidding me," Gary says. He shakes his head. "Makes you wonder, doesn't it."

He passes the plate of shrimp and Stevie takes one. She watches Joel, who picks empty beer cans from the laundry basket and begins to pitch them, one by one, out onto Gary's lawn.

"Joel," Stevie says, but Gary stops her.

"Let him be," he says.

After Joel has pitched the last empty can, Gary says, "I don't know where that wife of mine is. I guess I'd better go and check on her."

Gary goes into the house and Joel and Stevie are left alone on the deck. Stevie looks out at the beer cans scattered all over the lawn, and she sees a bright yellow golf ball in the grass.

"Look at that," she says, and she steps down from the deck and picks up the yellow ball.

"Give it here," Joel says, standing.

Stevie hands it to him through the deck railing, and he winds up and pitches the ball as far as he can toward the golf course. It disappears in the trees along the creek. She starts to pick up the cans and Joel says, "Leave them the fuck alone."

Stevie looks at him, stunned by his voice and the anger directed at her. He says, "If it wasn't for you, I would've been there. It might not have happened."

She tries to believe she was mistaken, that she didn't hear right. She knows she did, though. Her hands start to shake and she drops the cans on the lawn. She wants to scream at him, say something terrible that will go deep, draw blood. Then Joel is over the deck railing, flying over the rails, landing in the soft grass in front of her. She takes a step back, but he grabs her and holds her tight. She can feel his hand in her hair, a fist, his face in her hair, and he says, "I'm sorry. Jesus, I'm sorry."

Stevie holds him and says, "It's all right, Joel." She says, "It's like the jacket, if it had only been a few inches longer."

Gary comes to the patio doors and sees them. He looks a bit uncertain, but he says, "I suppose we might as well eat."

Joel lets Stevie go. He bends to pick up an empty can.

"Without Lynn?" Stevie asks Gary.

"We can just start," Gary says. "I don't know what's keeping her, but I'm starving. What do you say? You as hungry as I am?"

"I don't mind waiting," Stevie says, stepping back up onto the deck. "Don't feel we have to eat right away for me. I could have another glass of wine while we wait for Lynn."

Gary fills her glass again and she sees Lynn's wine glass, still empty on the table.

"Let's be honest here," Gary says suddenly. "I don't imagine she's coming out. Don't take it personal. She doesn't come out for anybody anymore."

"Would she come out if just Joel was here?" Stevie asks. She wants her voice to sound matter-of-fact, but of course it doesn't.

"If she would, I think Joel should drive me home."

"No. That wouldn't make any difference," Gary says. A hot gust blows across the deck and threatens to lift the white cloth right off the picnic table. Lynn's empty wine glass tips over.

"Aren't we a bunch tonight," Gary says, catching the glass just before it rolls off the edge of the table.

"Let's eat before we blow away in this wind," Joel says, stepping back up onto the deck with a half-dozen empty cans. He puts them in the basket, then takes a paper napkin from the picnic table and wipes off the toes of his boots.

Stevie goes inside to get the salad and this time she looks down the hallway and tries to guess where Lynn might be. There are two closed doors, one on either side of the bathroom at the end of the hall. She steps quietly onto the hall carpet and, not daring to stop in front of the closed doors, switches on the bathroom light and closes the door after herself. She listens, placing her ear against the wall, first on one side and then the other. She hears nothing, no television, no radio, no hair dryer. She checks the bathroom counter, which holds the usual cosmetics and bathroom products, his and hers, and the medicine cabinet, which contains nothing but a bottle of Aspirin and a box of plastic Band-Aids. The bathroom is spotless and a pair of guest towels hangs above the sink. She flushes the toilet and runs the tap for a minute, then goes back to the kitchen, stepping quickly back down the hall.

The radio in the kitchen catches her attention again as she tosses the salad. The announcer says the weather watch has been upgraded. The conditions are now right, he says, for the formation of funnel clouds. People should be on the lookout.

Stevie takes the salad and the news out to the deck. The sky is beginning to darken.

"What should we do?" she asks as she puts the salad on the table.

"Just keep our eyes open," Gary says. "But don't worry. We might get funnel clouds all right, but they hardly ever touch down."

Joel pulls a beer from the cooler and says he's going to phone his mother at Anne's in case they haven't been listening to the radio.

"That's good," Gary says after Joel has disappeared into the house. "Joel looking out for his mother like that." He helps himself to salad and motions for Stevie to do the same. She does, and they watch the golfers. Most of them are heading toward the clubhouse, some on foot, others riding on their carts. Apparently someone has spread the news about the weather warning. Gary gets himself another beer and says maybe he should light the barbecue coals, but then he doesn't. They watch the sky grow blacker and the golfers hurrying toward the clubhouse. The temperature drops and Stevie shivers. Gary notices.

"You need a jacket?" he asks.

"I should have brought mine, I guess," she says. "I thought it was going to be one of those hot nights."

Gary goes in the house and brings her back a jacket, a beautiful hand-beaded jean jacket, Lynn's.

"Where's Joel?" Stevie asks, putting on the jacket.

"He's still trying to reach his mother," Gary says. "The line seems to be tied up."

"This is a beautiful jacket," she says, running her fingers over the beaded patterns.

"She bought that in South Dakota," he says. "We used to travel a lot. Just head out with the camper for a week or two. We went all the way to New Mexico once. Lynn wanted to go there because of the artists. You should see the work the artists do in New Mexico."

Gary fills Stevie's glass again and she knows she should stop him but she doesn't. There isn't much wine left in the bottle.

"Lynn wanted to be an artist," he says. "Did you know that?"

Stevie nods.

"She told me once, after one of our trips down through the States, that if she came back in another life she wanted to design cowboy boots. She'd just bought a pair in Great Falls. Tony Lamas, beautiful boots. After we got home she started drawing designs with coloured pencils in a sketch book. She still does, once in a while."

"Maybe she could sell them. Her designs, I mean," Stevie says.

"I don't imagine there's much call for boot designs," Gary says.

"I don't believe you should ever wait for another life," she says.

"That's youth talking," he says. "Anything I haven't done has to wait for a new life."

"You're not old," she says. "And besides, a new life might not come. You can't count on it."

"It doesn't take much to make you old," he says. "The blink of an eye and a few low blows. You'll find that out soon enough."

"I hope not," Stevie says. But then she says, "Joel's with Lynn, isn't he."

Gary nods.

She starts to cry. She can't stop herself.

Gary says, "Oh Jesus," then he gets up and leaves her alone. He goes through the patio doors into the house.

Stevie despises herself for crying, because she's not the one who should be crying. She sits alone and calls herself an idiot, and then Gary's back wearing his jacket and carrying his car keys.

"Come on," he says. "Let's get out of here."

They step down from the deck and walk around the side of the house, where Gary takes her arm and leads her to his car.

And now everything seems normal, even though it isn't, driving with Gary across the bridge to the golf course side of the creek and up behind the clubhouse, where he parks. They walk out onto the golf course and up Devil's Hill, climbing the north side to avoid the mass of cactus plants. When they reach the highest point, they can see the whole sky, the town below them, the golf course, Gary and Lynn's house. Stevie worries momentarily about the tornadoes, but the dark clouds are mostly to the east now. Gary sits down on top of the hill and she sits beside him. They watch the sky.

"I don't think this storm is going to come to anything," Gary says. "It's going to blow on by. The golfers will be back out before you know it."

The wind is blowing stronger on the hill, and Stevie pulls Lynn's jacket closer around herself. Then Gary says, "Lynn and I come up here at night sometimes, after it's dark. She says it clears her head."

"Do you understand her?" Stevie asks, hoping her question doesn't sound too young and naive.

"I like to think I do," he says, "but maybe I don't. It's possible that I don't understand her at all."

There's a long silence and then Gary says, "So you work for the competition."

"Just for the summer," Stevie says. "I'll get laid off when the tourist season is over."

"Tourism doesn't affect me," he says, "not being on the highway. I have my regulars, that's what keeps me going."

"It hasn't been that good this summer at Jake's," she says. "The road construction's kind of cut into his business."

"Guess it's been a bad summer for Jake all around," he says. "I feel sorry for him, even though I hear he was a mean old bugger to work for."

"I wouldn't know," she says. "I only met him once. He interviewed me for the job, then that weekend was the accident. His son was already running the place when I started." She stops, and then she goes on. "One thing I know. He's got someone stealing from the till. Someone who works there."

"That's tough," Gary says. He pulls his jacket collar up against the wind. "I've had that happen. I can trust Joel though. I'd trust Joel with anything."

"I know who it is," Stevie says.

"That's a difficult situation," he says. "Are you going to turn him in?"

"Yes," she says. And now that she's said it out loud, there doesn't seem to be any other way. "I guess I will. I guess I'll phone Jake Jr. in the morning."

"Jake will appreciate that," Gary says.

"He'll call the police, won't he?" Stevie says.

"I imagine he will," Gary says.

"I'm embarrassed about crying back there," Stevie says. "I haven't had anything bad happen to me, not like Joel."

"You're just worried about him," Gary says. "Don't worry about what he was saying earlier, about Amos Quinn. Joel isn't going to do anything stupid."

"That wasn't it," Stevie says. "I was crying about myself. I'm embarrassed to say so, but that's the truth."

"You're good for Joel," he says. "I mean that."

"I think I am," she says, "but who knows. I might not be. I might be all wrong."

"What do you think the future holds for you and Joel?" Gary asks.

"It's hard to say," she says. "I'm planning to go to back to school. That's as far as I've thought. Joel doesn't know yet."

"Lynn and I got married when she was just seventeen," Gary says.

"I know that," she says.

"I've got no regrets," he says. "Lynn claims to have none. But you never know. You never know how things could have been different."

"I just hope I'm not making a big mistake," Stevie says. "I feel I have a lot to lose. Joel, I mean."

She sees a little patch of white at her feet, a patch of tiny white flowers growing so close to the ground they remind her of lichen on a flat rock. She touches them and they're dry, straw-like. They feel dead, but still they're pretty, like dried flowers from the florist's.

"Look at these," she says. "I've never seen flowers like this before." She moves her feet so Gary can see the flowers. "What do you think they are?" she asks, and when he doesn't answer she looks at him and realizes he's crying. She's never seen a man cry before, not even Joel when Derrick died. She stares.

"I'm sorry," Gary says. He puts his head down on his arms and sobs.

Stevie moves over close to him and puts an arm around his back. This doesn't seem to be enough, though, so she slips her hand inside the upturned collar of his jacket where she finds warm skin. She rubs the back of his neck until the sobs stop and his breathing returns to normal.

"I'm sorry," Gary says again. "I don't know what came over me."

"I guess it's just a night for crying," Stevie says. She pulls her hand away then, and leans her head on his shoulder and feels the cold, black leather of his jacket against her cheek. "We'll watch out for them, won't we," she says. It comes to her lips easily, even though she doesn't know whether it's possible or true, at least in her case, because she has decided and now there's no turning back.

Leon's Horses

Esther Lubyk lived at the end of the line on the old Stretton place, about two miles into the hills past Ada and Leon's new house, the one Leon built after the fire. The road to Esther's went right by Ada's kitchen window, so Ada couldn't help but notice any vehicles that passed, as long as she was home, and she usually was. Most vehicles coming up the road were headed for Ada and Leon's. It wasn't very often that one went by on its way to Esther's.

The first time Ada saw the red Ford truck pass her window in the early evening she didn't give it much thought, other than to wonder who it was, and then to note that whoever it was didn't make the return trip until after eleven. When she saw the same truck go by a second time on the way to Esther's, she paid closer attention. She tried to get a look at the driver. She could tell it was a man, but she couldn't get a good look because her kitchen window faced west and the sun was setting behind the hills, turning everything a brilliant red. It was just that time of day, and it made Ada think of the hills on fire.

As she watched the truck disappear to the north and Esther's for the second time, she thought, "There is only so much the human heart can bear." She made a fist with her hand and studied its smallness. She held her fist to her chest, imagined her small heart beating away inside of her. She imagined Leon's heart, bigger than hers, beating more slowly the way a man's does.

When Leon got home at ten o'clock, he found Ada at the kitchen window, watching.

"Don't know what you expect to see out there," Leon said.

"Black as pitch tonight."

"Still," Ada said, "you can see headlights from a long way off."

"Expecting company?" Leon asked.

"Of course not," Ada said. "Not at this time of night. Company at this time of night can only mean bad news." She stared into the blackness. She could barely make out the horizon line as it followed the contours of the hills. She thought she could see something moving.

"Got any supper for me?" Leon asked, sitting at the table.

"You know, Leon," Ada said, "sometimes I think I can see your horses out there in the night."

"What I'd like to see," said Leon, "is a plate full of potatoes and roast beef on the table in front of me."

"I see them walking in a line along the hilltops," Ada said. She turned away from the window and took Leon's plate from the oven where she'd been keeping it warm.

"Which one's in front?" Leon asked as Ada put his plate on the table.

"What?"

"My horses," Leon said. "When you see my horses, which one's leading them along? If it's not Babe, it's not my horses you're seeing." He loaded his fork with meat and potatoes and took a mouthful. When he'd swallowed he said, "Madonna would be next, after Babe. Behind her, I'm not sure. Brandy maybe. Or Miss Kitty."

"I can't tell you what order they're in," Ada said. "All I can make out is the movement." She sat down at the table and poured herself a cup of tea. She was wearing a new pink sweater and she waited for Leon to notice it. She hardly ever wore pink. She thought of pink as a colour for younger women, but this sweater had particularly caught her eye.

"Where were you today anyway?" she asked him.

"Auction sale," Leon said.

"Buy anything?" Ada asked.

"Nothing much," Leon said.

"I know what that means," Ada said. "You bought some more junk. You bought another one of those surprise boxes."

"Two, in fact," Leon said. "I haven't unpacked them yet, so I don't know if there's anything good in them."

"Honest to Pete," Ada said.

"You'd be surprised what I find in those boxes," Leon said.

"They fill those boxes just for you, Leon," Ada said. "When they think you might be coming to an auction they get a box and fill it with all the stuff no-one in his right mind would buy."

"Nice new sweater, Ada," Leon said, getting up from the table.

"It's different, isn't it," Ada said, pleased that he'd noticed.

Leon watched the news on TV after he'd eaten, his bad leg resting on a footstool. There was a metal plate in his leg where a horse had rolled on it and crushed the bones, and sometimes it ached. Ada did up the dishes, and then she waited by the window again. Leon went to bed. Eventually, Ada gave up and crawled in next to him. He was still awake.

"Bought a horse today," he said.

"What?" Ada asked. She sat up and switched on the bedside lamp. She needed to look at his face to see if he was telling the truth.

"Bought a horse at the auction sale," Leon said, shielding his eyes. "Turn that damned light out, will you."

"I thought maybe you were pulling my leg," Ada said, switching the light off and lying down again. "I guess you weren't."

"Sad looking excuse. I got her for seventy-five bucks though. Any bred mare has to be worth that."

"Well," Ada said to Leon, "I guess you know what's best." She wasn't sure he did.

"I'll throw up a lean-to at one end of the corral," Leon said. "She'll be okay there until I can get a barn built." He paused. "Don't expect too much. Like I said, she's a sorry looking excuse."

Ada sighed. "There is so much sadness in the world," she said.

"The grass has come back pretty good in the east pasture," Leon said. "I guess we're lucky on that account."

"You're not thinking about going back into the horse business, are you?" Ada asked.

Leon laughed. "Not with this mare," he said. "Wait till you see her."

They lay side by side and Ada could feel Leon moving his pillows around, readjusting his shoulders, shifting his hips, first one way, then the other.

"Do you want me to rub your back?" Ada asked.

Leon threw back the covers and rolled over onto his stomach. Ada hiked up her flannelette nightie and straddled him, most of her weight on her knees, which couldn't take it like they used to. She kneaded from Leon's shoulders down to the small of his back, but she had to cut it short.

"Aren't we just getting old," Ada said. "Older and older."

"Time passes," Leon said, then he went to sleep. Ada heard the truck go by. She listened to it fading into the distance, feeling quite certain it would come again, not knowing whether that was a good thing or bad.

Ada could think of no word to describe what had happened to Esther Lubyk. Sad? Tragic? Sorrowful? They were all inadequate. In any case, it was the worst thing that had happened to anybody Ada had ever met, and a lot of bad things had happened in the district over the years. Like when old Mrs. Carlyle went outside to get wood one winter night and fell and froze to death before morning. Or when the two teenaged girls from town were killed when their car rolled on graduation night. Or the Milner boy getting paralysed when he went head-first off his horse trying to wrestle down a steer at the Maple Creek Rodeo. And Leon losing his horses four years ago in the big fire. Yes, Ada thought, even though they were just horses. But nothing was worse than Esther Lubyk losing all of her children and no-one to this day knowing for sure what happened.

Esther hadn't lived on the Stretton place then. She'd lived south of the river with her husband. The children, three of them, had drowned in the dugout. Their clothing was found at the edge of the water, folded in neat little piles as though they'd gone swimming. But Esther had insisted they would not have. They had all been drilled time and time again on the dangers. The oldest was twelve and a responsible boy; he would not have let the two little ones go in the dugout. So what had really happened to Esther's children, what circumstances had taken the three of them down the muddy banks and into the black water, remained a mystery.

Ada had known the Lubyks to see them, but not well enough to share in their grief. People went to the funeral from all over the country, Ada heard, people who had never laid eyes on the Lubyks. They had gone to gawk, the way people came in droves to gawk at the remains of Ada and Leon's lives after the fire. Ada refused to be one of those people. She was ashamed for them.

Inadvertently, though, she *had* ended up a voyeur. She saw Esther in town a few weeks after the funeral, looking through picture frames in the Co-op store. She wanted to say something to Esther, but she hadn't been able to think what. She cursed herself for being so bad at such things and more or less hid in the kitchen wares section listening to Esther talk to Mrs. Tooney, the clerk.

"I want the frames school-picture size," Esther said. "Five by seven, I think. The youngest didn't go to school, but luckily I had her picture taken at the mall in Swift Current last Christmas. You can order pictures the same size as school pictures."

"I see," Mrs. Tooney said. "Well, we have these nice brass ones. They're plain, but elegant."

"They're very pretty," Esther said. "I'll take them if you think they're the right size."

"You can bring them back if they're not," Mrs. Tooney said.

They took the frames to the counter.

"It's something I always meant to do," Esther said. "Buy nice frames for the school pictures."

Ada watched as Mrs. Tooney wrapped the frames and Esther got her wallet out of her purse, and suddenly Mrs. Tooney burst out, "I can't take your money for these frames, Mrs. Lubyk. I simply can't. Please. Take them. It's only right."

Esther looked startled. She murmured something that Ada couldn't hear, picked up the frames and quickly left the store. Ada waited a few minutes, then went to the counter and paid for a half-dozen packages of freezer bags because she thought she should buy something after spending such a long time in kitchen wares. She tried to pretend she hadn't overheard and said, "Lovely summer day, isn't it," to Mrs. Tooney, but it fell flat, and Ada ended up leaving the store as quickly as Esther had, without even saying thank you.

A year later Esther split up with her husband and rented the Stretton place at the end of the line on Ada and Leon's road. When Esther first moved in, Ada went to visit her, just to be friendly. The fire hadn't reached that far north, and as Ada drove into the yard she saw that the place looked pretty much the way the Strettons had left it. The old two-storey farmhouse still stood, along with the barn and a few outbuildings. She noticed a cow and calf watching her from the small pasture west of the house. The pasture was nice and green. She heard a horse whinny from inside the barn.

She found that Esther was decidedly unfriendly. Ada would have got back in the truck and gone home right away, but it was awkward. She stood in the yard, wondering how to leave, saying things like, "My, I haven't been up this road in years," and, "I'd forgotten about these apple trees. Old Mrs. Stretton used to make a wonderful apple pie," until finally Esther offered her a cup of coffee. Ada accepted with relief, even though she knew she wasn't really welcome, and handed Esther a plate of brownies that she'd brought with her.

Esther led the way inside the house, which appeared to be in decent shape even though it hadn't been lived in for several years. The walls looked freshly painted. When Ada sat down at the kitchen table, she was able to see into the living room. It was poorly lit, but she picked out the three shiny brass frames on the wall above the couch.

Ada tried to drink her coffee quickly, and whenever there was an awkward silence she told Esther another story about the Strettons, knowing full well that Esther could care less. She felt silly eating her own brownies when Esther ate none, but untouched they seemed to call attention to themselves. She told Esther that the recipe had been her mother's and was committed to memory, a good thing too because when she'd been throwing things together to take away before the fire reached the yard, she hadn't thought of her recipe books.

"A fire like that would be bad," Esther said.

"Not *as* bad," Ada said, and then there was another awkward moment.

As soon as Ada finished her coffee, she stood to leave. She tried to get Esther to keep the rest of the brownies, but Esther insisted that Ada take them home with her, so she did. Esther walked her to the truck and just as Ada was about to open the door, Esther said, "I appreciate your thoughtfulness. I don't mean to be rude."

"Of course you don't," Ada said. She blushed because of Esther's directness. It came so unexpectedly.

"A marriage can't survive the death of its children," Esther said. "At least mine couldn't. There was just nothing left." Esther looked at Ada. The look wasn't unkind, but it wasn't friendly either. It wasn't an invitation.

"The reason I came here," Esther said, "is that being alone is the only way for me to survive now. I know that to be God's truth."

"I understand," Ada said, knowing that she was being asked not to come back.

And she never had been back. They'd said hello on the street in town a few times, and Esther phoned Leon once in a while for help with something. A year or so after Esther moved onto the Stretton place, Ada heard that her husband had remarried. He still lived south of the river. When the red truck started making trips in to Esther's regularly, Ada remembered her saying, "Being alone is the only way for me to survive." Ada couldn't help but worry.

Leon had to borrow a horse trailer to bring his new mare home because he hadn't replaced his own trailer after the fire. Although Ada had been able to save some of her most precious things, Leon hadn't saved anything because as soon as he'd heard the fire was coming he headed out into the hills, looking for his horses.

Ada went outside to watch him unload the black mare. She was an ugly horse, swaybacked, with warts all over her nose. She was skinny, even though her belly was swollen, and she had an open sore on her withers. It was a hot day and she was already attracting a swarm of flies. Leon got Ada to hold her halter while he put some ointment on the sore and rubbed her down with an insecticide to keep the flies from driving her crazy. Ada wanted to touch the mare's nose, but she couldn't bring herself to do it. The warts were too ugly.

Leon watered the mare and turned her loose in the corral, which he had thrown together after the fire and then never used. He broke open a bale of hay that he'd carried from the trailer and tossed a few flakes over the rails.

"She should foal in six weeks or so," he said. "She might work out all right as a brood mare. You never know."

"You haven't put up hay since the fire," Ada said. "You'll have to buy a load."

"I don't think I'll bother trying to ride her," Leon said. "She doesn't look like much of a riding horse."

Ada thought, she doesn't look like much of a horse at all, but she didn't say it out loud. She was too puzzled. Leon had never owned such a horse.

The red truck passed on its way to Esther's two or three times a week. Ada was in the habit of fixing herself up after supper and she often saw the truck go by from her bedroom window, which, like the kitchen window, faced the road.

Fixing herself up after supper wasn't anything Ada had done all her life. She had started doing it rather late in life, in fact, and hadn't thought much at all about her appearance when she was younger. She hadn't really noticed her own body until it began to look old, and then she wished she'd looked at it closer before. She thought maybe she should have appreciated her looks more while she still had them.

When she first started to think about her appearance, she just fixed her hair a bit and made sure she didn't have gravy or raspberry juice splashed on her blouse. Soon she began getting dressed up, just a little, in a white blouse and pants maybe, or her blue dress, the one with tiny cream-coloured flowers on it. She wasn't sure why she did it, but it became a ritual that she looked forward to. One thing she knew, she liked it when Leon noticed, which he usually did.

"You going out?" he asked the first time he saw that she'd changed her clothes.

"No," she said. "I just had a notion to fix myself up a bit."

Her fixing herself up became the object of much teasing by Leon and some of the other neighbours as well, especially the men. Leon was always threatening to take her dancing, but she knew he never would because of his bad leg.

Whenever Ada saw the truck go by in the evening while she was washing up the dishes or putting a little rouge on her cheeks, she worried. She knew, though, that what went on between Esther Lubyk and her frequent visitor was none of her business. She had to believe that Esther knew what she was doing, just like she had to believe Leon knew what he was doing keeping that sorry horse in his corral. Even though she wasn't sure he did.

Ada dreamed that Leon was riding his new horse. She dreamed

she was watching them head right into the fire at full gallop.
Black smoke billowed up along the horizon and the wind blew it
toward her, making her draw deeply for breath.

Leon was calling back over his shoulder as he rode.
"Adaaaaaaaa!" he called. She tried to answer but she couldn't get
her breath and the roar of the fire kept taking whatever sounds
she made.

Leon tried a few different salves and ointments on the sore on the
mare's withers, but none of them seemed to work. It wouldn't
heal, and she developed a slight fever. Ada was reading zucchini
recipes in a magazine at the kitchen table when Leon came into
the house and asked her to put in a call to the vet.

"Ask him if I should haul her in, or if he's planning to be out
this way sometime soon," Leon said. "Tell him there's no rush. If
he's coming this way, I can wait."

Ada looked at Leon over her glasses, a look that clearly said the
horse wasn't worth the cost of a vet's visit.

"Just call the vet, Ada," Leon said, and went back outside. Ada
did call the vet, and he said he would be out their way on Friday
and he'd drop by.

"So Leon's back in the horse business, is he," the vet said.

"I'm not sure," Ada said. "I'm not sure what he's up to with
this horse."

Leon kept a lookout for the vet's truck all day Friday, but he
still wasn't there by supper time so Ada and Leon went ahead and
ate, and then Ada fixed herself up for the evening. She changed into
a skirt and blouse, put on just a hint of eye make-up, which she had
recently begun doing, and screwed some silver-coloured maple
leaf earrings onto her ear lobes. She sprayed a little perfume behind
her ears.

"So," Leon said when she came from the bedroom. "You all set
to go dancing?"

"I'm just taking a little pride," Ada said. "There's nothing
wrong with that."

The vet pulled into the yard and parked down by the corral.
Leon went out to meet him and Ada sat down to play a game of
solitaire at the kitchen table. She heard another vehicle coming up
the road, and when she went to the window she saw that it was the

red truck on its way to Esther's. The truck went past, then slowed, stopped and backed up to Ada and Leon's approach. It turned in and then disappeared behind the house.

Ada hurried to the back door and looked out. The truck was heading for the corral where Leon and the vet were examining the horse. Ada could see the driver now, but she couldn't tell much about him. He looked like a big man. He was wearing sunglasses so it was hard to say how old he was.

Ada watched as he stopped the truck, got out, and climbed over the corral rails. She quickly opened the door and crossed the yard, her heart beating with the certainty that she was going to get a good look at Esther's visitor. The men were laughing at Leon's horse, she could hear them as soon as she got near.

"You should have bought yourself a sawhorse," the stranger was saying.

"Don't be so quick to laugh," Leon said. "A twenty-five-dollar horse is not to be laughed at."

"Going to cost you a damn sight more than twenty-five dollars for this doctoring," the vet said.

They noticed Ada. She stayed outside the corral, as she wasn't going to climb over in her good clothes and there was no gate, you had to unstack one section of the rails.

"Hey there, Ada," the vet said. "Don't you look nice. Must be stepping out on a Friday night."

"Not unless I can get Leon to take me somewhere," Ada said. "He's always talking about dancing, but he's all talk."

"Too old for that kind of thing," Leon said.

Ada sneaked a look at the stranger. "You told me that horse cost seventy-five dollars, Leon," she said. The stranger still had the sunglasses on. They were mirror glasses. He was facing west, and the sunset was reflected in his eyes.

Ada thought, his eyes are all on fire.

"Ada," Leon said. "How many times have I got to tell you that when it comes to horse business you ought to keep your mouth shut."

"I'm just trying to protect these two gentlemen," Ada said. She turned to them. "You can't believe a word he says when he's talking about how much he paid for a horse."

They all laughed, even Leon. The vet saw Ada looking at the stranger.

"Ada, this is Mervin Jakes," he said. "He's from south of the river. A mean bugger. That's why he wears those glasses. They cover up his mean steak."

Mervin Jakes took off his glasses and looked at Ada through the rails.

"Nice to meet you," he said. Ada didn't recognize him from anywhere.

"South of the river," she said. "That's Esther's old part of the country."

"That's right," Mervin said.

Ada guessed him to be about forty years old. Other than that, he didn't give anything away. She looked down at the glasses in his hand. The fire had disappeared.

"Well," Mervin Jakes said, turning back to the men. "I'd best be hitting the trail. I just thought I'd stop to ask the doc here when he's going to be in the south country again. I'm awful damned glad I stopped. Otherwise, I wouldn't have had a chance to see this horse of Leon's. She's a sight to behold."

"You'll be laughing out the other side of your face a few weeks from now," Leon said.

"I'll give you a call sometime next week," the vet said to Mervin Jakes.

Mervin climbed back over the rails and Ada watched him get in his truck. Before she could stop herself, she was walking toward him. Mervin saw her coming and rolled down the window.

"Now look here," Ada said to him. "I know this is none of my business, but Esther Lubyk doesn't need any more sorrow in her life."

Mervin Jakes looked past Ada. He had the sunglasses on again and she couldn't tell what he was looking at.

"I appreciate your concern," he said finally. "I'd like to be able to say you don't have to worry, but I can't do that. It wouldn't be honest. I've known Esther a long time. I guess that's about all I can say."

Ada stepped away from the window. She nodded and Mervin reached for the ignition and turned the key. He drove out of the yard and north to the Stretton place.

Ada went back to the house. After the vet left, Leon came in and Ada asked him about his horse.

"I've got a prescription here that ought to fix her up," Leon said. "Hard to say for sure though." He sat down at the table while Ada plugged in the kettle and got a bag of Dad's cookies out of the cupboard.

Ada dreamed she was on Leon's black mare. The fire was burning in the hills, burning so bright she could hardly stand to look at it, and Leon was out there looking for his horses. Ada tried to get the mare to run in the direction Leon had gone, but she wouldn't budge. She stood quivering, like she was trying to shake the flies off on a hot summer day. Ada kicked her sides. The mare grunted with each kick, but she wouldn't move. Ada hit her with a willow switch and an open sore appeared. Then she realized the horse was shivering with fever. She felt the horse's legs begin to give.

"Leonnnnnnnn," Ada yelled into the fire.

The fire burned and flashed along the hilltops.

Leon woke up because Ada said his name out loud.

"What's the matter?" he asked her. It was still dark.

"Nothing much," Ada said. The dream was fading quickly. Already she was having a hard time remembering it. "I was just dreaming about your horse."

"I know she's an eyesore," Leon said, "but I didn't think she'd give you nightmares."

"Never mind," Ada said. "By the way, you did tell me you paid seventy-five dollars for that mare."

"I never said any such thing," Leon said. "You must have heard wrong."

Ada knew there was no point arguing. It was something she remembered from before. Nonetheless she said, "I heard right." She moved up against him. "I guess this means you're back in business."

Leon was quiet for a long time. Finally he said, "I think I'll order up the materials for a new barn tomorrow. That ought to keep me busy for a while."

Then he rolled over and Ada knew he was going back to sleep. She lay for a long time thinking about the way the fire flashed in the hills, and about the fire reflected in Mervin Jakes's eyes, how it was there and not there. She heard his truck coming down the road from Esther's place. Leon's horse whinnied from the corral as it passed.

Big Otis and Little Otis

I REMEMBER the time the three of us were in the grocery store and Nick touched me and Audrey got mad. Nick and I were standing in the breakfast cereal aisle laughing at the names on the boxes: Captain Crunch and Count Chocula and the like. Nick must have leaned forward to point something out to me, and as he did he put his hand on my arm. Audrey came around the corner and saw, and for the rest of the afternoon she wouldn't speak to either of us. We had no idea why. She told me later that night, after Nick had gone home. I convinced her she was being ridiculous and then we had a good laugh about it. She told me that's what happens when you're in love with someone. You become insanely jealous, she said, and assume every woman finds your lover as attractive as you do. I remembered some of the men I'd thought I'd been in love with. It hadn't occurred to me that any other woman would want them. I decided I hadn't really been in love, at least not as in love as Audrey was, and I took her word for it that insane jealousy was a sign of true love. I assured her I definitely was not attracted to Nick and she accepted that, although she said she found it hard to believe I could resist him.

That was when Audrey and I were living together, before she moved in with Nick. We lived in the attic of a big old three-storey house owned by John and Christina Papandreos. John was older than Christina. She was probably the same age as Audrey and me, and had just come over from Greece and couldn't speak English.

She had a baby the first year we lived there and while she was in the hospital John had a party to celebrate. Audrey and I were listening to the laughter coming up the stairs, when we heard footsteps. It was John, and he invited us down for a drink. Audrey didn't want to go because we'd never been invited into the Papandreos living room by Christina. It was Christina's living room, she said, and we shouldn't be there with John and a bunch of men while Christina was in the hospital with a new baby.

"How do you know there won't be any other women there?" I asked Audrey.

"All I can hear is men," she said, listening at the top of the stairs.

"That's because male voices carry," I said, and I managed to convince her we should go down. We got dressed up because John had been wearing a dark suit and polished shoes.

As it turned out, Audrey was right. We were the only women. We sat side by side on straight-backed chairs and John served us small glasses of ouzo. Christina's living room walls were covered with framed photographs of Greece, and all the coffee tables displayed photographs of happy families, some with three or four generations posing together. All the furniture in the living room was draped with squares of lace – the overstuffed chesterfield, the tables, the fireplace mantel – and I imagined the lace was an heirloom that Christina had brought with her.

The men in the room were all older than we were. They were dressed in dark suits like John's, and spoke Greek much of the time and laughed heartily. I felt like I was a part of a ritual, but I wasn't sure what to say or do. I smiled whenever the men laughed. Although it was disconcerting, I pretended to understand perfectly.

Audrey, I could tell, was extremely uncomfortable. She asked about the baby, and John showed us the hospital pictures. When we finished our glasses of ouzo John went to pour us another, but Audrey stood up quickly and said we had to be going.

"He won't tell her we were there," Audrey said after we were back upstairs. "She'd kill him."

I didn't believe that, and I couldn't see why Audrey was being so suspicious. It clearly had been an innocent celebration of a birth.

Audrey and I lived in that house for two years, then she moved into Nick's apartment with him. I was seeing a man named Roger at the time, and I considered asking him to move in with me to save money on rent, but when we split up three weeks later I was glad I hadn't. I resigned myself to living in John and Christina's attic alone.

The summer that Nick and Audrey moved in together, they announced they were going to build a log cabin on a leased piece of land Nick had in the north. Their apartment was soon littered with how-to books on log building, and every time I went to visit them they'd have a new floor plan drawn up and ten reasons why this plan was better than the last one. Audrey told me the cabin had been a dream of Nick's for a long time, but that he hadn't been able to commit himself to it until he met Audrey who, it turned out, had a similar dream.

"I've never known you to be remotely interested in wilderness living," I said to her, and she told me there were some things about her that I didn't know.

"For example," she said, "I don't imagine you know that I like avocados. Avocado and German butter cheese sandwiches are my favourite. On five-grain bread."

I had to admit I didn't know that. When we lived together, her favourite had been Cheez Whiz on Wonder bread.

"Well," I said, "I suppose we're not too old to develop new interests. And I don't mean to be critical. Building a log cabin sounds great."

"Maybe you can help us next summer," Audrey said. "We're hoping to get a lot of people to help, so it goes faster."

Nick learned from his research that you should cut your logs the year before you want to build so they can dry out and shrink. That fall he went north for two months while Audrey stayed behind to work and save money. He got the logs cut, poured some concrete pillars for a foundation and even laid the floor joists. He came back full of enthusiasm, and all winter he and Audrey talked cabin and pored over photographs of the lake and the building site. I spent hours with them drawing floor plans and looking at coffee table picture books on handmade houses, and after a while I started to feel like I had a vested interest in the cabin, like it was part mine, even though I knew that was ridiculous.

When spring came, it was assumed that I was going with them for the summer, and of course I did. Christina was good and pregnant again when I left. She still couldn't speak English, but she smiled at me and waved as I went out the door with my tent and duffel bag. John promised they would keep my room for me, and was nice enough to charge me only half the rent for the months I was away.

We were twenty-nine, all three of us, that summer. We had jobs, but not jobs we were committed to, and we were more than willing to quit and take our chances again in the fall. We went north in May and Nick recruited a half-dozen people besides me to come along and help.

Nick's lease was on a quiet bay. The building site was on a hill right above the lake shore, and the cabin was to face the water. We left our cars at a public campground and got to the lease by boat, that's how private it was. You could even skinny-dip, which we did later in the summer, but in May the ice had just gone from the lake and it was too cold.

The first thing we had to do was peel the logs. It would have been easier if they were freshly cut with the sap still under the bark, but Nick had cut them after the sap was down and now the bark was stuck to the wood. We all complained, Audrey the most bitterly and with every pull of her draw knife, but she kept at it even after the others, me included, had given up. She told Nick that he'd made a mistake in letting the logs dry out, but he insisted they were better that way and claimed they'd end up a nice dark colour because they were dry.

When it came to peeling logs, Nick had a big advantage over the rest of us. He liked a physical workout and was in good shape from lifting weights at the YMCA. He was actually worried he was going to lose his build over the summer, so as soon as we'd got to the lease he'd rigged a chin-up bar between two trees. Every morning he jumped rope or ran on the spot for forty-five minutes while the rest of us drank coffee and watched him. Later, when the water in the bay warmed up, he started swimming two miles a day.

Had his friends been as interested in fitness, they might have lasted longer. As it was, they lasted a week. Or should I say Audrey tolerated them for a week. There was a raft anchored in the bay and after they gave up on log peeling, it became the favoured spot for all-night parties. When Audrey saw we weren't going to get much work out of the crew drinking beer on the raft, she got really bitchy and refused to feed them and everybody packed up and left.

Everybody but me. It wasn't that I liked peeling logs any better than anybody else did. I hated it. My reason for staying had more to do with Audrey not living in the attic anymore, and Audrey and Nick being together, and me never having had a man in as permanent a way as Audrey now had Nick.

We lived in two tents. Audrey and Nick had a big white canvas bush tent, which they'd strung between two trees fairly close to the fire. It was big enough to stand up in, big enough to make cosy. They built a platform bed inside so they weren't sleeping on the ground, and they stacked some wooden crates to make a sort of dresser and bookshelf next to the bed. They burned candles at night. I had a two-man nylon pup tent that I pitched a respectable distance away, but I made sure I could still see them in case I was attacked by a bear in the night.

The pup tent had a floor and could be zipped up tight so I didn't have to worry about mice or insects getting inside. Audrey and Nick were always finding spiders in their clothes and once Audrey threw a hysterical fit in the middle of the night because she was sure a mouse had run right across her face.

Sometimes it wasn't much fun being there. At least Audrey and Nick knew they were building something for themselves, but me, I wasn't sure what I was building. In truth, I was tearing down, doing a pretty decent job of destroying my friendship with Audrey. I was moody and argumentative much of the time. Once I told Audrey that I didn't think she and Nick would last. I said he had no sense of humour, which wasn't even true, but I wanted to point out to her that Nick was not as much fun as I was. And once I went so far as to say I thought men who spent so much time thinking about their bodies did so because they didn't have much confidence in their brains. Anybody but Audrey would have sent me packing, but Audrey knew me well enough to know I didn't mean half the things I said. At night I was lonely and Audrey knew that too, although I tried to hide it by saying I was fed up with men. I announced one night after several beers around the fire that I was considering turning Catholic and becoming a nun. Nick thought that was pretty funny and I said, "Laugh all you want. But I'm serious. I mean it. I really do." Audrey just told me I was full of shit and went to bed, leaving Nick and me alone, which she didn't seem to mind doing, even though she'd got so mad when he touched my arm in the grocery store.

"I don't know what's got into her," Nick said, which was when I knew the complexities of female friendships were beyond him.

At times, in spite of my gloomy state, I was glad to be there. By the middle of June the lake was warm enough for swimming, at least the top of the water was. If you let your legs hang down so you were perpendicular it was so cold it took your breath away. Still, it felt good after working all day, and we'd go down to the bay for a swim in the late afternoon. Sometimes, if it was especially hot, we'd take a long break at noon and lie in the sun. Nick could carry things out to the raft by holding them above his head and swimming with just his legs. He'd take a radio out that way, and a beer for each of us. We could have taken things in the boat, but it was fun to watch Nick and wonder if he could really make it without sending whatever he was carrying to the bottom of the lake. We used to joke that Nick was like Atlas, the Titan son of Mother Earth. After Nick unloaded the loot, Audrey and I would lie nude in the sun and bake and listen to the CBC while Nick swam his two miles in the bay. When he was done, he'd climb onto the raft and we'd all lie in the sun. I'd watch Audrey and Nick, study them, trying to figure out what was different about their relationship from any that I had ever had with a man. They were easy together. That was the main thing.

In the evening, we'd sit around the fire and eat fried jackfish fillets and canned corn or peas, and listen to the radio. It was our only way of keeping in touch with the outside world. That summer the CBC was playing old radio dramas like "The Shadow" and "Ozzie and Harriet," and they ran something called the "Airwaves Personal Classifieds," where people could phone in their personal want ads and they'd play them on the air. What hit me every night was the number of people advertising for partners. Audrey and Nick listened to the men who called in and tried to decide which ones would be good partners for me, which kind of bugged me because I didn't think I was that needy. They thought it was a joke.

Most nights, I'd lie in my tent with the flaps open, my sleeping bag facing the screened door, and look out at the dark for a while before I went to sleep. Sometimes Audrey and Nick would have a candle burning in the tent. I could see their shadows. Sometimes I knew they were making love, even though they always blew the candle out first.

I began to see them as a permanent couple. I wondered whether they'd get married and if they'd have a real wedding in a church, and I thought about what they'd look like middle-aged and whether or not they'd have children. This led me to wonder if I would ever have children, and one night when I was lying in my tent it occurred to me that, even though I was alone and had no immediate prospects for a male partner, I could have a baby. Why not? Lots of women raised children on their own, some of them intentionally. Once the idea was there it was hard to get rid of, and I often went to sleep thinking about it.

The work on the cabin was not going all that well. It took us over a month to peel all the logs and that put us two weeks behind schedule. After the logs were finally peeled, we started building the walls. Neither Audrey nor I knew how to use a chainsaw and neither of us particularly wanted to learn, although I pretended I did. Nick had two saws, and he went ahead with the building while Audrey and I practised on some scrap end pieces. After a week or so we both knew how to fire up the saw and hollow out a corner notch, but when Nick suggested he do all the intricate sawing because he was faster, Audrey agreed. I put up a bit of a fight just for show, but really I was as willing to go along as Audrey. I kept thinking the saw was going to kick back and hit me in the face.

Nick had worked out this fancy way of cutting a V in each log and stuffing it with fibreglass insulation. The V was supposed to allow the log to fit perfectly over the one underneath it, but for it to work you had to do this accurate marking with callipers all along the length of the log. Audrey and I would do that part, then Nick would saw along the marking. The system didn't seem to work. The logs kept getting hung up on knotholes and when Nick tried to fix them he'd cut so much away that there'd be nothing left. Audrey would blame Nick for sawing wide of the mark, and Nick would blame Audrey and me for marking inaccurately. But we kept plugging away. By the end of June we had only two rounds down and we'd ruined four logs, a full round. Nick was beginning to worry he hadn't cut enough.

As June turned into July, the idea of me having a baby as a single woman had really taken hold and I tried to convince myself it wasn't a stupid one. I was twenty-nine. Time was passing. In fact, I told myself, it was running out and I hadn't had what you would call a date for six months. As I watched Audrey and Nick, I felt like their kind of relationship, their kind of easiness, was too far in the future for me. I didn't want to wait.

One night I dreamed I was lying very close to Nick on the raft. He had his back to me. Audrey wasn't there, and I was desperate for Nick. I kept inching closer to him until we were finally touching. When he felt my body next to his, he turned toward me and placed his hand on my abdomen. It was like fire, but pleasantly so. I lay beside Nick and absorbed the heat. I didn't want him ever to take his hand away, but he suddenly stood, dove into the water and swam away from me. I tried to ease into the water to follow him, but it was too cold. Steam rose from my belly when the cold water touched it, and I quickly climbed back onto the raft. I looked for Nick, but the whole surface of the lake was covered with a steamy mist and I couldn't see him. I woke up, and lay for a long time in the dark thinking about Nick.

For days afterward I couldn't look at Nick without remembering how badly I'd wanted him in the dream. If he caught my eye, I'd look away. I could hardly have a conversation with him. I worried that I was acting guilty, but I must not have been or Audrey would surely have confronted me.

Gradually, the dream faded and began to seem embarrassingly silly. My wanting Nick was once again replaced by the desire to have a baby. The dream, though, led to other, more clinical, carnal thoughts about Nick. I decided he could be the father of my baby. At the time, it seemed logical enough.

Nick was up at the camp doing the dishes after supper one night and Audrey and I were sitting on a rock near the water's edge when I came out with it. Audrey gave me the strangest look. I'd thought she might be angry, but this was a look I didn't recognize.

"I can't believe you're asking me this," she said.

"It's not that I feel anything for Nick," I said, convinced that this was true. "Nothing more than friendship. But I thought that might be the best way. If I tell you there'll be no responsibility in the future for you or Nick, you can believe me, because we're friends. I mean, I'm not going to call you up and ask for child support or anything like that. Do you see what I mean?"

"You're asking me if you can borrow Nick," Audrey said.

"I suppose you could put it that way," I said.

"You know," Audrey said to me, "I'll be glad when you hook up with somebody. You are a really stupid single person. You need somebody to straighten you out."

That cut fairly close to the bone. I began to feel stupid. And then defensive.

"What are you saying?" I asked. "Are you saying I'm not able to look after myself? Are you saying I'm not a complete person on my own?" I was trying to turn things around so that Audrey would look at least a little bit as stupid as I felt. "In this day and age," I said, "I thought it would be possible for two women to have a mature conversation about a sensitive topic without resorting to name calling."

"I'm going to help Nick with the dishes," Audrey said, getting up. "I'm going to pretend that this conversation never took place."

"You're jealous again, aren't you?" I said. "Like the time Nick touched me in the grocery store."

"For Christ's sake," she said, turning away from me and starting to walk up the hill. "You are incredibly ignorant if you can't see the difference between the two incidents."

"I wouldn't exactly call this an incident," I said, rationalizing like mad. "It's more like an innocent request made of a best friend."

Audrey stopped. She appeared to be thinking, then she came back and sat down beside me again. I waited for her to speak.

"*I'm* trying to get pregnant," she said. "I've been trying ever since Nick and I moved in together and nothing's happening. So how am I going to feel if you and Nick do it and you get pregnant? Besides that, I don't want you and Nick to sleep together. I just don't want you to. There. That's my end of a mature conversation about a sensitive topic."

"Oh," I said.

I stared down at the water awhile, then I asked her why she hadn't told me she was trying to get pregnant. Audrey didn't say anything. I stared at the water awhile longer, and realized that I didn't want to have a baby, not the way Audrey wanted to.

"I didn't tell you because it's between Nick and me," Audrey finally said. "Some things are just between Nick and me. You'd understand that if you'd ever had a long-term kind of relationship."

At that moment I had a hard time believing Audrey and I were the same age. I felt like I was her daughter.

"I don't want to go for a bunch of stupid tests," Audrey said. "I don't want them poking around and treating me like an infertile white rat. That's the next step, you know. Nick's already checked out fine."

A loon called across the lake. I could hear Nick rattling dishes in the camp above us.

"Maybe you could adopt," I said.

"Nick doesn't want to," Audrey said. "At least not yet. He wants me to have the tests and see if there's anything can be done. He's big on natural childbirth and all that. He wants us to have a home birth and he'll be the one who catches the baby when it's born."

"Gee," I said. "I didn't know Nick was such a romantic."

We sat for a while longer, then I told Audrey I was sorry I'd had such a dumb idea and asked her not to tell Nick.

"Don't worry," Audrey said. "He'd probably want to oblige you. I won't mention it."

"Me wanting a baby was just a whim," I said. "When I see how badly you want to be pregnant, I know it was just a whim."

"You're lonely," Audrey said.

"Let's not talk about this anymore," I said.

"It's in the past," she said. "It's fading from memory."

"Good," I said.

"It's gone," she said. "I can't even remember what we were talking about."

We walked up the hill to the camp and the radio classifieds were on. Nick had already written down the address of some guy named Otis in Salmon Arm, British Columbia. He handed me a slip of paper.

"He's tall, considered good-looking by some, reads a lot and plays the trombone," Nick said. "He's just what you're looking for."

I put the slip of paper in my pocket.

"Oh yeah," Nick said. "He's a single parent. Could you handle that?"

"She can handle that," Audrey said. "You'd be surprised how well."

Later that night, while we were sitting in the dark watching the embers, Audrey started to laugh.

"Otis," she said. "Big Otis and Little Otis."

"What?" Nick asked, looking at me as though it must be a private joke. I shrugged and looked at the fire. Audrey kept laughing and ended up with an all-out attack of the giggles. I couldn't help it. Pretty soon I was laughing as hard as she was. Nick was left out. It was like old times, me and Audrey, best friends. Nick kept trying to get us to tell him what was so funny, and that just made us laugh harder. After we went to bed, I could still hear Audrey laughing in their tent. It was comforting. With a clothespin, I attached the slip of paper with Otis's address written on it to a line I had strung across the inside of my tent.

The next day, and from then on, there was something between Audrey and me, like a stone in your shoe that you can't seem to shake out. I got the feeling she didn't like it when Nick and I were alone together. At first I thought she would get over it like she had the grocery store incident, but one day she attacked me after Nick and I had been fishing. We were down near the water where Nick was filleting a big jack on the flat end of a canoe paddle while I watched. He had the sleeves of his denim shirt rolled up and he slit the belly of the fish with the deftness of a surgeon. Audrey came walking along the shore carrying her sketchbook and singing to herself. She stopped when she saw Nick and me.

"Have you told him what you're up to?" she asked me.

"What?" I asked.

"You know what I mean," Audrey said. "Rock-a-bye-baby."

"Audrey," I said, embarrassed. "I thought that was forgotten."

"On my part, but apparently not on yours." She went to the tent and didn't come out for supper.

"What was that all about?" Nick asked.

"I don't know," I lied.

The next morning I asked Audrey if she wanted me to leave. I didn't really want to, but I thought if Audrey didn't want me there I should go. She said she wanted me to stay. She might have just been feeling sorry for me, but I stayed anyway. After that, things between us got a little better. At least she didn't accuse me of anything again and I didn't think she'd said anything to Nick because he was just the same as ever, and regularly wrote down names and phone numbers from the airwaves classifieds for me. I ended up with a collection of men clipped with the clothespin in my tent.

Audrey's birthday was at the end of July. She was the first of us to turn thirty. She woke up cranky, and I thought it was maybe because of some goal she'd set for herself that she hadn't met, like she was going to be pregnant by the time she was thirty. Nick asked me if I thought we could bake a cake over the campfire. I said we could probably make a kind of airtight stove out of a tin bread box we had. It was a hot day and we told Audrey she couldn't work because it was her birthday, and she had to spend the entire afternoon on the raft. This was so we could rig up the stove and surprise her with the cake. She got Nick to swim a book and the radio to the raft for her, then she stretched out in the sun on her stomach.

Nick and I mixed up the cake. We piled some rocks in the fire and balanced the bread box on them, then put the cake inside, punched a hole in the lid for a vent, and closed it up. It was ingenious enough, but the first cake burned black. We decided that we had the fire stoked too high, so we let it burn down to hot coals and tried again. While we were waiting for the fire to die down, we swam out to the raft. Nick took Audrey a cold beer from our stash in the lake. She told him she was sick of lying in the sun, but he told her she had to stay there because we were making her a surprise. Audrey looked at me, almost pleading, but I went along with Nick and told her it was a great surprise that would be ruined if she came anywhere near. I was thinking of the smell of the cake baking.

The second cake was burned on the bottom, but not bad. We cut the black off and decorated it with pieces of canned fruit. Nick got a candle from his and Audrey's tent and stuck it in the top. Then we carried it down to the shore and called Audrey. She was asleep on the raft. Nick decided he could swim the cake to the raft, so he stuck some matches on top of it and started out. He swam on his back, holding the cake above him, gliding after powerful kicks, and I swam along beside him trying not to splash. When we were just about there, Nick dropped the cake. He'd been trying to turn over onto his stomach so he could lift the cake up to the raft, when it slipped out of his hands. I shrieked when I saw it fall and Audrey woke up. She was sunburned. Her cake was making its way slowly to the bottom of the lake, disintegrating as it went, and Nick was shouting at her to hurry up and at least get a look at it. Audrey watched the cake sink, then looked at Nick and me and started to cry. Her skin was lobster red. I didn't know what she was crying about, but I suspected it was because Nick and I had been together all afternoon while she was on the raft getting skin cancer. I turned and swam back to shore, leaving Nick to sort it out.

I went to my tent and lay on my back, bathed in the strange blue light that came through the nylon tent walls, feeling terrible. I reached up to flick a moth off my clothesline, and I accidentally knocked down all the little classified ads. Otis from Salmon Arm landed on the pillow next to my head.

Salmon Arm. I'd never been there. Maybe, I thought, I should drive to Salmon Arm for a holiday. Maybe I could just kind of give Otis a call, arrange to meet him for coffee or something. I wondered if that would be a dangerous thing to do, but after having his name in my tent for several weeks I felt like he would be safe. And he was a fellow CBC listener. Dangerous people wouldn't listen to the CBC. They'd listen to some country and western or heavy metal station.

Audrey was in their tent when I left, smeared with Noxema and propped against a rolled-up sleeping bag on the bed, reading a novel. I stuck my head through the flaps and told her I was leaving for a few days.

"Fine," she said, without looking up. "See you when you get back."

"Yeah," I said. "See you then."

I got Nick to take me in the boat back to the campground where I'd left my car. For the first part of the half-hour trip we didn't talk, but then Nick said, "Audrey thinks we should go ahead with it."

"What?" I asked, not understanding at first.

"You know," Nick said. "It. Have you been taking your temperature? If you knew when you were ovulating we'd probably only have to do it once or twice and we'd have a take."

I figured out what Nick was getting at, but I couldn't bring myself to talk to him, at least not about that.

"I'm on my way to Salmon Arm," I said.

"Salmon Arm?"

"Yeah. You know. Otis. Considered good-looking by some. Trombone player."

"Oh," he said. "You're actually going to do that?"

"Yeah," I said. "So if you never see me again, give Otis's name and address to the police."

Nick cut the motor on the boat and we coasted to the dock. I was glad to see my car was still in one piece in the parking lot. I climbed out of the boat with my gear and Nick waited to make sure my car started, then he waved and pushed the boat away from the dock, heading back to Audrey. I remembered her crying on the raft, and I hoped she was pregnant and her crying was a symptom, some kind of hormonal mood swing.

I decided not to wait to get to Salmon Arm before phoning Otis. I called his number from a phone booth at the first gas station I came to. A child answered the phone.

"Hello," I said. "I'm a friend of Otis's. From out of town."

"He's not home," the child said. "But you can come over and wait for him."

"How long will he be?" I asked.

"He's bowling. But he should be home soon. I cooked supper for him. There's lots, if you want to come."

"Oh, I couldn't do that," I said.

"Why not?"

"Because," I said.

"That's not a very good reason," the child said.

The child was right. There was no good reason why I shouldn't head for Salmon Arm. But I didn't. I went home to my own apartment and got there just in time to watch John load Christina into the car and take her to the hospital to have her second baby. This time there was no stag party in Christina's living room, I supposed because John's mother had come to look after John and the two-year-old while Christina was in the hospital. For some reason, I was saddened by this and I went to the liquor store and bought my own bottle of ouzo, which I sat on my bed and drank, enjoying the heat that settled in my belly. I thought about inviting John to sneak past his mother and share the bottle with me, but of course I didn't. I thought it was too bad Audrey and I weren't one person instead of two and then everything would be fine.

The Evidence

ALL Saturday afternoon Marty waits at the motel. He passes the time by watching an NBA game on television, the Celtics versus the Knicks. His station wagon is angle-parked just outside the door to his room, its licence plate number beckoning any officer of the law who happens to be cruising by. After the incident at the old couple's place this morning Marty considered heading back to Calgary, where he keeps an apartment, but then he decided, what the hell, let them pick him up here and be done with it. He's looking forward to getting it over with.

He lies on the double bed, two flimsy pillows behind his head, and curses motels that don't put extra pillows in the closets. The first half of the basketball game is good – fast and smart, lots of defensive action. But in the second half it begins to look like the Celtics, who just aren't the same without Larry Bird, are going to fall apart. Marty thinks what a shame it is when a hot team's players start to get old and he decides he doesn't want to see the final score. He flips the channels around and finds a game show where people go on blind dates and afterward tell the world what a good or terrible time they had. This amuses him for a while, but it's soon over. A program about different breeds of house cats comes on next. He hates cats. He turns off the TV without checking any other channels.

He wishes they'd hurry. He has a ground floor room and the curtains are wide open so he can see when they pull up, which they're bound to. Maybe there'll be a whole bunch of them. Maybe they'll bring the SWAT team and surround the motel and evacuate everybody in case he has a gun. He hasn't, of course, because he isn't a real criminal.

Propped against the alarm clock on the night table next to the bed is a Polaroid snapshot of Marty and a tiny, white-haired old woman sitting close together on a couch. He has his arm around her. They look funny together, Marty being a big man and she being so wizened and pencil-thin. He examines himself in the photo, tries to scrutinize himself with a completely objective eye. He is draped around the woman, comfortable, relaxed, smiling a big goofy smile. He could be anybody, he decides, anybody close, until you look at her and see how frightened she is.

He'd told her she looked like his mother and insisted that her husband, an equally frail and aged man, take their picture together. In fact, the woman looks nothing like Marty's mother, who is strong as a horse and still dyes her hair flaming red at seventy-eight. Marty doesn't know why he's keeping this evidence against himself at such close range. If he were a real criminal, he'd be afraid of getting caught.

Saturday night. The police still haven't picked Marty up, so he drives across the street to a bar called Bud's & Ricardo's. He could have walked, should have for the exercise, but it's not convenient to walk along this strip of motels, gas stations and fast-food drive-ins. Everything here is designed for cars, for transience and quick stops. Pedestrian crosswalks are few and far between and there's no way Marty is going to try to dart through four lanes of traffic. Besides, he wants his station wagon close to wherever he is because that's what will identify him, what the police will be looking for. He parks in a conspicuous spot under a light standard and climbs the stairs to the bar above the motel restaurant.

A young band called Major Rock is playing, not rock as you'd expect from the name, but some kind of weird hybrid that's unfamiliar to him. The band has a conga player and there's a primitive quality to the music, a disturbing edgy kind of sound. Marty's over forty, close to fifty in fact, but he's always prided himself on keeping up with the music of the day. He picks up Top 40 tapes for the road and he reads the odd issue of *Rolling Stone* or *Billboard*. His travelling leads him to spend a fair amount of time in bars, and keeping up on rock music seems like a professional responsibility, or if not that, a survival tactic, since he's always tried to avoid the kind of place where middle-aged men like him are fixtures, where he'd get too comfortable listening to the piano stylings of Honey So-and-So, back by popular demand. Until recently, he seemed to understand what was going on with rock music, at least nothing surprised him. But lately – well, it's turning into a language he doesn't understand. He's beginning to feel like he's in a foreign country.

Still, he picks places that have bands instead of piano bars, places like Bud's & Ricardo's. He can't see very well in here because the lights are dimmed, but Bud's & Ricardo's looks like an okay spot, lively at least. He orders his usual brand of domestic beer, the one he's been drinking for over twenty-five years, then he situates himself at the back of the room so he can check the place out. He leans against the wall and strains to see in the darkness. The crowd is mostly young, it appears, and he decides that Major Rock must play pretty good music. He comes to this conclusion the same way he decides by listening that someone must speak pretty good French, even though he himself can hardly speak a word. Major Rock sounds fluent, and people in the bar look like they're having a good time. He tries to get into the spirit by nodding his head and tapping one foot.

The band is loud, annoyingly loud, and Marty has to yell when the barmaid walks by. He yells when he asks her to marry him, and she takes his empty glass and yells back. She's already married, she says, and besides, she's promised Charlie that if she ever splits with her husband she'll marry *him*. She points out Charlie. Marty looks. At a table not far away he sees a guy at least as old as he is. The guy is more than a little overweight and almost completely bald. The barmaid laughs as she pushes past Marty with her tray of empty glasses and Marty thinks, this barmaid is a nice person. There *are* some of them left. A few. But not many. From his observations of late, the world has gone to what his ex-wife Hanna would call rack and ruin. Or hell in a handbasket. That was another of her favourites. Hanna. Now she was a real doom-sayer. Heavy Hanna, their friends called her, and they weren't referring to her size.

Hanna believed, and explained tirelessly to whoever would listen, that the whole world had a brain the size of a chicken's. Her theory, which had something to do with collective consciousness, caused Marty nothing but embarrassment when they were still together, but he's come round to thinking that there could be something to it. Now that he's in the same ballpark as Hanna on this, he wonders whether they might possibly be able to have a conversation if they should run into one another. Perhaps they could, although they both might have to go out and slit their wrists afterward.

He keeps looking at the door, waiting for some burly cop to come in with his name written on an official slip of paper. A warrant? He's never been arrested before, but he's watched a lot of TV. They'll read him his rights, but he already knows he doesn't need a lawyer or a phone call.

His neck gets tired from craning every time someone opens the door. He wonders where old Heavy Hanna is now. Probably converting people somewhere to her particular brand of religion. Last time he saw her she was heading off to Bible school. That was twenty years ago, before either of them had turned thirty. They had never actually got divorced, so Hanna couldn't be married to anyone else and Marty still has a wife, technically speaking. That gives him something to think about. He wonders if the nice barmaid is really married.

This thing Marty gets into with barmaids is just a game, but he does think someday he might get lucky. Not lucky as in sex, although he likes sex a lot, but lucky as in love-you-forever, although that's getting to be a long shot and he knows it. And as much as his flirting with these barmaids is a game, he truly admires them, their incredible tolerance for chaos and the way they give themselves over to people. Of course, some barmaids are as mean as junkyard dogs, but he avoids those ones. In truth, they scare the bejeezus out of him.

This particular barmaid is what Marty calls a superior woman. She's wearing a silky, forest green blouse that he would love to touch, and she has the most amazing smile. She's not that young, she'll never see thirty-five again, but age isn't important to him. Well, obviously it is important because he's thinking about it all the time these days, his own age anyway, but he's not one to be fussy about a woman's age as long as she takes care of herself.

He looks at his competition again. The guy's belly is literally hanging over the top of his pants. The longer Marty looks at him, the bigger he seems to get. Marty is a few pounds overweight, sure, and definitely out of shape, but he's not that big. He likes to think he could still be considered attractive by someone like the barmaid in the green blouse. She really is amazing, laughing and talking to people as she takes their orders and delivers drinks. Marty watches her, he can't take his eyes off her.

His attention, though, is suddenly drawn to the music. There's something about it, this particular song, that seems familiar from away back. What is it? He listens carefully, trying to catch the lyrics. "Witchcraft," that's it, an old Frank Sinatra tune, but Major Rock is not doing any rendition that Marty has heard before. The singer is growling out the words as though he's in a horror movie, and dry ice vapour begins to sift up from under the band's platform. And what's the conga player doing? Jesus. His erratic rhythms are affecting Marty's heartbeat, he's sure of it. He finds himself wishing they would just do the song the way Sinatra did it, and at the same time he can't believe he's thinking this, he hates nostalgic covers of old tunes. He hates, for example, Harry Connick Jr., who's hitting the big time with his blatant imitation of Old Blue Eyes. Harry Connick Jr. even sang the American anthem at one of the World Series games last year. Now there's a measure of success, but why didn't they just ask Sinatra himself? Marty remembers the last picture he saw of Sinatra. He'd gained a few pounds. Quite a few, in fact. At the time Marty had found the famous crooner's weight gain reassuring. Now, with these jungle drums violating a once respected song, it just seems depressing. He could cry for Frank.

Then the song is over and the nice barmaid brings Marty another beer and he wonders what got into him for a few minutes there. He laughs right out loud. Did he really think he was ready to curl up in an armchair and listen to the *Best of Frank Sinatra?* The barmaid smiles. Marty puts his arm around her like they're old friends and tells her it's too bad he's so far back on the waiting list. He sees the other guy, Charlie, watching him. Maybe, he thinks, Charlie is jealous. That makes Marty feel good. Charlie is sitting with three other guys, all with their bellies hanging over the tops of their pants, all looking older than most of the other clientele, and every once in a while one of them says something and they all stare at Marty. Marty leans against the wall, nonchalantly holding his beer glass so that his ring finger shows. He's wearing a real diamond.

Now what is Major Rock doing? One of the guitar players is singing, you can see his lips move, but damned if Marty can hear a single vocal. The conga player is working himself into something downright primeval and the guitars are squealing like there's a big problem with the amplifiers. Why do they do that, these young bands? And how can people dance to this garbage? Then Marty catches himself, he's sounding so old, and he decides to go with the band on faith, whatever it is they're doing, whatever it is he doesn't understand. Bud's & Ricardo's is hopping and this, after all, is what Marty came for on his last night of freedom.

What possessed him this morning, Marty can't really say. Maybe it had something to do with Dr. Lorenzino. If he really was a doctor. Marty had his suspicions. Although Marty refused to believe that the so-called doctor could possibly have affected his conscious mind, it is possible that he could have worked somehow on his subconscious.

According to Dr. Peter Lorenzino, who had spent two days last week trying to teach Marty and seventy-four other salesmen how to come up with creative ideas to increase their sales at least tenfold, almost everybody in the world has a very efficient, well-oiled left side of the brain. The other half of the brain, however, is in trouble. Dr. Lorenzino spent the first few hours of the workshop proving all seventy-four right brains in the room were in serious trouble.

"And science tells us," Dr. Lorenzino said, "that creative ideas are born on the right side of the brain. What I am going to give you is exercises for bringing your right brains back from the atrophied state they are in. Call it physiotherapy for the mind, if you will."

"What's this got to do with sales?" Marty asked the fellow salesman sitting next to him.

"Don't you get it?" the man said. "It's a classic." Then he went on to explain that Dr. Lorenzino was like the snake oil salesman who convinced his listeners they had some dreaded disease, then pulled out the cure and sold it to them at two bits a pop.

"It cost my company a lot more than two bits to send me here," Marty said.

"Of course," the other salesman said, and looked at Marty as though he felt sorry for him.

"So is this helping you any?" Marty asked. "I mean, does the right side of your head feel any better?"

"No," he answered. "But look, you gotta respect the guy. It's a hell of a concept."

They spent the rest of the workshop coming up with creative ways to do things like market ice cream in the winter and sell obsolete railway cars. The only thing Marty learned was that seventy-four people in a room can come up with a lot of stupid ideas.

What Marty had done to the old couple this morning was stupid, no doubt about that, just as stupid as any selling idea that had come out of that room. But when he thought about it, really thought about it, he didn't think he could blame what he'd done on the two days he spent with Dr. Lorenzino. No, whatever the reason Marty had done what he did, he had to admit that it probably had nothing to do with sales.

He'd pulled into a farmyard not unlike a thousand other farmyards, and the dog barked and the lady of the house looked through the kitchen window, then answered the door. Up to that point, everything was just as usual.

But when Marty explained what he was selling and the lady said she didn't need any more magazines because she picked up all the ones she wanted at the drugstore in town, Marty kind of flipped. He actually pushed his way into the house, sat down at the kitchen table and told the woman to make him something to eat. Something to eat for Christ's sake, and he wasn't even hungry. The woman was old and he frightened her and he knew it. It turned out the woman's husband was asleep on the couch and when he heard Marty talking he woke up and wobbled out to the kitchen, leaning on a cane. Marty asked him if he had any cigarettes, and when the man stared at him blankly Marty jumped up and pounded on the kitchen table and said something like, "I need a smoke and a plate of food and if I don't get it I'm going to set your goddamned house on fire." It was incredible, really. He couldn't believe he'd done it. And as soon as the woman got the tobacco can down out of a cupboard, Marty started feeling shitty. The woman's hands were shaking so badly she could hardly roll the cigarette. The old man looked like he'd stopped breathing. Marty badly wanted to tell them he didn't mean it, he was really a decent person, but when the woman went to the fridge and started pulling bowls of food out of it, Marty flipped again. He wanted to say, "No, no. I was just joking. Bad joke. I'm not going to set your house on fire." But all he could get out was, "Sit down and relax." And they didn't sit down. They stood staring at him, both of them looking like they'd stopped breathing, so he had to yell at them again and tell them for Christ's sake to sit down. So they sat down, and then Marty felt even worse than before. That's when he told the woman she reminded him of his mother. He'd never treated his mother very well, he said. Not that he was proud of it, but that's the way it was and there wasn't any changing it now. He'd meant that to calm the woman down, but then she said, "I'll fix you some dinner, just don't hurt us," and that was the last straw. Marty picked up the fruit bowl that was on the table in front of him and threw it across the room. It hit the wall and broke and oranges and apples rolled around on the kitchen floor. The old man still hadn't said a word. He looked like he didn't know what was going on, which of course he couldn't have because even Marty didn't know, and the old woman put her arm around her husband protectively.

"Why is he here?" the man asked his wife.

"He's selling magazines," the woman said. He was hard of hearing and she had to shout into his ear.

"Did you buy any?" the man asked.

"Not yet," she shouted.

"Maybe you should," the man said.

"Do you want me to buy some magazines?" the woman asked Marty. "Is that all you want? Just tell me how many. I'll buy as many as you want me to."

Marty imagined Dr. Lorenzino patting him on the back, congratulating him for coming up with such an effective sales strategy. He started to laugh and the old couple cowered on the other side of the table until he finally stopped. When he could talk again, he told the woman to get his Polaroid camera for him out of the station wagon, and she did and didn't even try to drive away and get help. Marty got the old geezer to take the picture of him and the woman on the couch. In fact, he got him to take two, and he gave one to the woman after signing his name on the front like a movie star: "Best wishes, your friend Marty." He wrote his car license number on the back, XLJ 227, and left the house.

There were chickens all over the yard and they scattered as Marty drove through them on his way out. When he hit one, he could have cried. Then he remembered someone, maybe it was Hanna, telling him chickens have no brains, just nerve endings. It was probably true. Chickens, he thought, were without a doubt stupider than, say, ants. To have a brain smaller than an ant, well, it wouldn't be worth having one at all. That made him feel better as he left the farmyard and turned onto the gravel road, but then the real pain of what he'd done caught up with him and he had to pull over. He sat with the window rolled down, gulping air, until he was able to start the station wagon again and head for the city.

There's only one empty table in Bud's & Ricardo's, which Marty hasn't claimed. He doesn't want to look like he'd welcome company, and that's what empty chairs at your table say. He chooses to remain standing. That way, he reasons, he looks like he's alone because he wants to be. He looks interesting as opposed to desperate.

He wonders about Charlie and his three pals. They must be local boys. Travellers are usually alone, unless they're at a meeting or a convention. Or unless they've picked up a hitch-hiker. Marty doesn't pick up hitch-hikers anymore. Too many other travellers he knows have had trouble.

Charlie is wearing a white V-necked sweater with nothing under it but a heavy gold chain. He can't keep still. He's sitting one minute and then he gets up and kind of dances on the spot for half a song. The next minute he's sitting again, looking thoroughly pleased with himself. Marty decides to move a little closer to Charlie's table so he can hear what they're talking about. During a brief interlude in the music, Marty hears one of them ask, "Hey Charlie. What are you so happy about?"

"Why wouldn't I be happy?" Charlie says.

"She's too nice to you," Charlie's friend says. "She's just being nice to you 'cause she feels sorry for you. You should thank your stars that such a nice girl will even talk to you."

Marty assumes they're referring to the barmaid. She walks by just then and Charlie says, "Hey honey, I'd love to play your bongos." Charlie lifts his eyebrows in a suggestive manner. Marty almost pukes.

"Oh Charlie," the barmaid says. "You're cute, but you're so predictable." She gives Charlie's bald head a quick rub as she goes by. Now it's Marty's turn to be jealous. He turns away, heading back to his spot against the wall. He's heard enough from Charlie. What an asshole.

It's almost midnight now and the cops still haven't come for him. He thinks about phoning the police station and giving them a hint, but before he gets around to it he finds out what the barmaid's name is and gets distracted. Her name turns out to be Myrna. Marty hears the bartender calling her to the phone. He watches her to see if he can guess who the call is from. She looks annoyed.

The musicians put their instruments down and get set to take a break. The bartender turns the lights up. The band has been playing on a plywood platform about two feet off the floor and it looks pretty makeshift now that you can get a look at it. There's a funny sort of mural painted on the wall behind the platform, which Marty notices for the first time. A pink convertible with no-one behind the wheel sits in front of a city skyline, a big city, maybe New York or Paris. He pictures himself driving the convertible, someone snuggled up close beside him, preferably someone in a silky green blouse. For a brief moment the painting gives him hope, makes him feel like he could be somewhere else, but then he sees the ragged edges of the canvas stapled to the wall and remembers he's always somewhere else and that's probably the biggest part of his problem.

He wants to say something to Myrna, but now that the band isn't playing it's more difficult. Why is that? Everything is more difficult when the band isn't playing. Maybe it's because, with the lights up, everyone can see that you're alone and you wish you weren't, that these nights almost always begin and end the same way. Christ, Marty thinks, why don't the police come and haul him out of here? Then this night at least would end with a twist.

Myrna comes by and asks him if he wants another beer.

"Yes," he says, trying to sound cheerful and upbeat, even

though he doesn't feel that way. "And I hope you had a humdinger of a fight with your husband."

"Now why would you want me to fight with my husband?" Myrna asks.

"Because then I'd be one step closer," he says. "Next in line after that guy, remember?"

"You're all such jokers," Myrna says, still smiling, although there's a funny edge to her voice now, like she too is tired of the nights beginning and ending the same way.

"What time do you get off?" Marty asks her.

"That's like asking what time does it snow," she says and walks away.

Marty doesn't get it.

After a bit Myrna comes back with his beer, and then the lights dim and the band starts into the last set, the lead singer yelling into the mike now. Marty checks the luminescent dial on his watch. He can't understand why they haven't come for him. Maybe they're waiting in the parking lot by his wagon. That would probably make more sense, especially if they think he's dangerous. He should leave and check it out, but he doesn't because he can't stand the thought of leaving before Charlie. They're into a competitive thing here and, as ridiculous as it is, Marty doesn't want to lose by leaving first. Besides, Myrna might agree to have a drink with him when she's done work, one for the road, you never know. It's happened before, although rarely with such a fine woman as Myrna.

They're looking at him again. Myrna walks by with empty glasses on her little tray and because they're watching him, Marty has to say something to her.

"If you won't let Charlie play your bongos," he says, "maybe you'd like to play my organ."

"What?" she shouts. "Can't hear you."

He says it again, louder, but just when he gets to the part about the organ the band slams to a stop and half the room hears. Marty looks around at all the faces, so pathetically young, staring at him. Although the lights are dim, he feels as though he's under a spotlight, feels like they can see him breathing. They're all ready to burst into gales, he knows it. They're all just waiting to see what Myrna will do.

What Myrna does is give him a little play slap on the cheek, just a tap really. All the same, the watchers snort and hoot. Myrna says to him, smiling, always smiling, "Don't be fresh," and then she walks to the bar. Marty looks at his audience and shrugs, flashes his ring for effect.

He decides he can't just stand there, not with these young faces looking at him like he's some kind of novelty item, so he follows Myrna to where the bartender is filling drink orders. Marty steps up behind Myrna, planning to order a rye and water for a change of pace, and waits his turn. She's talking to the bartender. The bartender knows Marty can hear what she's saying, but he does nothing to warn her.

She says, "If I have to put up with one more geriatric asshole panting in my ear I don't know what I'll do. I might shoot someone. Some nights I can take it, but tonight they're driving me fucking crazy."

The bartender looks at Marty and smirks.

Marty quickly backs away so Myrna won't see him, but it's too late. Myrna turns to see who the bartender is looking at and her eyes meet Marty's. Then Marty bumps smack into Charlie.

"Sorry," Charlie says. "Hope I didn't damage your organ." Charlie manoeuvres his shape around Marty and up beside Myrna. He drapes his arm around her forest green shoulder.

"Listen, Myrna honey," Marty hears him say. "The boys and I are calling it a night, but here's a little something for your pretty smile."

Myrna takes the little something, slips her arm behind Charlie's back and gives him a squeeze. When she releases him, Charlie leads his three-man entourage out the door.

Marty doesn't care that he won, that Charlie was the first to leave. He wishes, in fact, that he'd lost, that he was right now in bed across the street watching some late-night talk show, or better yet, down at the police station getting fingerprinted and locked up. He doesn't want to face Myrna. Maybe she meant him. Maybe? Of course she meant him. The asshole part is bad enough, but geriatric, that's humiliating.

He has to get out. He starts to make his way toward the exit, but here she is in front of him, smiling just like before.

"What can I get you now, big fella?" she asks.

The band starts up again and Marty can't stand to be there, but he can't walk away from her either.

"Nothing more," he tells Myrna. "That's it for me." He quickly gives her a twenty dollar bill, trying to keep his eyes off her, her shiny hair and her silky blouse.

Myrna slips her arm around his waist and gives him a little hug, just like the one she gave Charlie. Marty is so surprised he jumps. Then he is so happy he could cry. He feels his disgrace melt away and thinks, how did she know? How did she know just what to do? She could have ground him into the cigarette-burned carpet with the sole of her high-heeled shoe, but she didn't. Instead, she offered him a more or less dignified way out. He takes it.

But oh, what he longs to take is Myrna. As she pulls her arm away and squeezes by him, he feels her breasts brush against him, feels them through her thin green blouse. He watches her push through the crowd, walking backward to protect the drinks on her tray, walking backward until she's lost in the darkened room.

When Marty steps outside, he sees a blue and red flashing light. For the second time in less than five minutes he feels relief and gratitude, feels that things might be going right. Then he notices that a police officer is shining his flashlight in the window of a car that's not his. It's a big sedan and Charlie is driving. The officer looks at his driver's licence, shines the flashlight in the back seat, and waves Charlie on. He gets back in the police car and turns the flashing light off.

"Hey," Marty shouts across the parking lot. The cop doesn't hear him. Marty watches him take a cigarette out of a pack and light it.

"Hey," Marty shouts again, louder this time. He walks toward the car.

The officer looks and rolls his window down all the way.

"You talking to me?" he asks.

Marty walks up to the window.

"That's my station wagon over there," he says. He points.

"Beg your pardon?" the cop says.

"I believe you're looking for me," Marty says, pointing again to his station wagon.

"I don't think so, buddy," the cop says, beginning to look irritated.

"No," Marty says. "You don't understand. I'm wanted."

"Not by me," the cop says, "although I'll charge you with impaired driving if you get in that vehicle."

The officer flicks his cigarette ashes out the window and onto Marty's shoes. Marty stamps his feet. He doesn't want to get picked up for drunk driving. He wants to get arrested for the crime he committed.

"Use your radio," Marty says. "Call and ask someone about me."

"Call a cab, pal," the cop says. "Go home to bed." He tosses his cigarette butt to the pavement. "Step on that for me, will you."

Marty does. The cop rolls up his window and begins to pull away from him.

"You don't understand," Marty shouts after him. "I'm wanted. I'm wanted, for Christ's sake. That's my wagon. XLJ 227. I'm a fucking magazine salesman. You're looking for me."

The officer, shaking his head, leaves him standing in the parking lot and turns onto the busy street. Marty watches him disappear in the traffic.

He stands alone in the parking lot and listens to Major Rock's music, still coming from up above the motel restaurant. He doesn't understand. He doesn't understand anything. Maybe, he thinks, it's because he has no brain. Maybe he has only nerve endings, like chickens. He imagines his trial, the one that it looks like he might not have, a doctor testifying in his defence that he's missing his brain. But would that be a defence? Brain or no brain, he knows the difference between right and wrong.

He gets in his station wagon and drives himself back across the street. It occurs to him that maybe he doesn't understand anything because he's an asshole, nothing more than a big time asshole. Maybe he should just admit it. It wouldn't provide a legitimate defence, but it might offer an excuse. He'd be happy to know he at least had an excuse.

Maybe what he should do is go somewhere far away and try to start over. He could catch a bus to Vancouver and fly to Australia, or maybe Fiji. He knows a guy from highschool days who runs some kind of factory in Fiji. The local workers call him Boss.

Marty could go for that. But then he thinks he's too old. People don't start calling you Boss at fifty when you've never been called Boss before.

He opens the door to his motel room and crawls into bed without even taking his shoes off. He looks at the photograph of himself and his victim. He imagines her husband's finger on the camera trigger, his hands shaking as he tries to do what Marty has ordered. Marty wonders how the photo can be so clear, then decides he frightened the old man into stillness. They must not have called the police, he thinks. It's the only explanation for his still being at large.

He considers the possibility that the old people weren't really all that frightened, that they just put on an act for his benefit. He looks at the photograph again, though, and knows the woman is not putting on an act. Then he thinks maybe they didn't call the police because the incident was just another ordeal in a life of frightening ordeals, something to be denied and forgotten as soon as it's over. Marty imagines the woman picking up the broken pieces of her fruit bowl, picking up the oranges and apples and arranging them in a new bowl, retrieving the dead chicken from the road and turning it into the evening meal. He thinks about this for some time, fills in more details, and decides it is what happened. It's the worst possible scenario, but it is what happened.

He turns out the light. What, he thinks, has he done with his life?

Bad Luck Dog

THE YEAR I was sixteen, the year my mother died, we lived in Canada's Rocky Mountain paradise, Banff National Park. My father had travelled ahead of my mother and me and found us a little rented house in the townsite, which we moved into just before school started in the fall. We weren't tourists, although at Christmas that year my parents sent postcards with mountain scenes instead of Christmas cards. I remember them staying up late one night, laughing at the kitchen table, writing things like, "Having a wonderful time, food is fantastic, wish you were here." The postcards would have been my mother's idea, and I was glad to hear my father enjoying her little joke. He didn't laugh that often, even though he had sometimes dressed up as a clown and done tricks at my birthday parties when I was younger. He knew how to juggle and could make his ears wiggle. He had tattoos on his forearms and once, at a birthday party, he had given my friends and me a bar of soap and a washcloth and bet us that we couldn't wash them off.

The year we lived in Banff, my father had a job as an insurance agent, which he got because his brother, my Uncle Bob, worked in the company's head office in Calgary. The year before that we'd lived in Bixford, Saskatchewan, where my father was the grain elevator agent. That job came to end when the elevator burned down and the company decided not to rebuild. Before Bixford, we lived at Cochin Beach where we managed a store that went bankrupt, and before Cochin we lived in Meadow Lake. My father was a social studies teacher then, but he gave up teaching forever when he was wrongly accused of carrying on a relationship with a girl in the highschool. I knew who she was. She was four years older than me and had dyed blonde hair. She got pregnant and said the baby was my father's. She finally admitted that it wasn't true, but by that time my father had resigned, given notice on the house, and sworn he'd never step foot inside a school again.

My father used to say bad luck was a bloodhound with a nose just for him. When something went wrong, he'd say to my mother, "That dog is after me again, Cynthia." I remember her once saying, "Well, let's put the poison out and make an end of him," and my father told her it wasn't that simple. He talked to me about the dog after my mother died, saying it had got mixed up somehow and gone after her instead of him. I was only sixteen, but I tried to tell him that when somebody died it wasn't because of a bad luck dog. Even though I wasn't convinced.

My father liked it in Banff. On Sunday afternoons we used to drive out of town and look for animals – moose and elk and mule deer. Although there were signs all over telling him not to feed the animals, he always took a little bag of oats and was immensely pleased if he could coax a deer or an elk to eat out of his hand. Other families would watch respectfully, believing he had a special way with animals. My mother said he was setting a bad example, but he said the signs were intended for stupid people who would feed the animals things like buttered popcorn. Outsiders, he called them, as though he had been born and raised in the mountains. He used to tell a story that he heard at work about a tourist who put food on the seat of his truck and coaxed a bear inside. Then he got his wife to get in so he could take a picture of her with the bear in the cab of the truck. The bear, of course, attacked her.

"Now that was stupid," my father said. "A far cry from feeding oats to a gentle deer."

One Sunday afternoon, my mother and father and I were parked at a lookout spot a few miles out of town, taking turns with the binoculars, watching big-horned sheep manoeuvre on the rocky face of a mountainside. They were beautiful, like dancers stepping along the narrow ledges. When it was my father's turn, he happened to sight a pair of rock climbers in bright orange jackets. He was trying to explain to my mother and me where exactly on the face of the mountain they were, when he saw one of the climbers fall. Startled, he lost the rock face in the binoculars, and when he found it again, both climbers were gone. The three of us scanned the cliffs, but could see nothing but sheep.

"Are you sure, Fred?" my mother kept asking anxiously. My father insisted he had seen them.

We drove quickly back to Banff and the park warden's office. My father reported what he'd seen and where, but the warden said he had no record of climbers being in that area. He drove us to the sight in an official park vehicle, so we could point out the exact rock face, which my father did. The warden said it was a near impossible ascent. Only a handful of climbers had attempted it, and he would most certainly know if any were up there. He clearly did not believe my father had seen anyone fall, but said he would send a helicopter up to look anyway. We went home and waited to hear from him, and later he called to say that nothing unusual had been sighted.

My mother and father argued that night. I listened from my bedroom. My father called the warden pompous and said he was typical of people who have too much power.

"He's just a park warden," my mother said. "He's not a general in the army, for heaven's sake."

"You don't believe me either," my father said.

"What do you expect?" my mother asked. "They looked, and there was no-one up there. Face it, Fred. You made a mistake."

I went to sleep thinking about two rock climbers, maybe dead, maybe alive on a narrow ledge, or stuck in a crevice with just a sliver of light somewhere above them. She should have believed him, I thought. It was her responsibility.

For two weeks after that my father stopped daily at the warden's office to see if any climbers had been reported missing by friends or family. He called the RCMP. He pored over newspapers, the *Calgary Herald* and the *Edmonton Journal*, thinking maybe he would read of a mysterious disappearance. Perhaps the two had gone climbing without telling anyone, he speculated.

I helped him look. One evening, when we were both going through newspapers on the living room floor, my mother came in. She spoke to my father in a way I had never heard her speak before.

"Now you've got Meg involved in this," she said. "Are you

trying to make a damned fool out of her too?"

"I'm not a fool, Cynthia," he said.

"You are going to go through life doing foolish things," my mother said. "At least spare your daughter the humiliation you've caused me." She left the room.

My father slowly, neatly folded up the newspaper he'd been searching through. "I guess they'd be dead by now," he said. "There's probably no point keeping this up."

He got up off the floor and put the newspaper on the coffee table, then he sat on the couch. I did the same. There was a bowl of oranges on the coffee table and he picked out three and began to juggle them. His eyes followed the oranges. I thought of the rock climbers in their orange jackets, my father catching them on their way down.

"I don't think she had to get so mad," I said.

He said nothing, just kept tossing and catching the oranges.

My mother called from the kitchen for me to help her with the dishes. She washed and I dried. We were standing side by side at the kitchen sink and I said, "What makes you think you're right all the time?"

"Don't try to pick a fight with me, Meg," she said. "I'm not feeling up to it just now."

"I think you've never forgotten that girl and her baby," I said. "I don't think you believed him about that either."

She stopped washing dishes and stood with her hands in the sink. They seemed to float up in the soapy water until they lay on the surface like dead white fish. She didn't look at me. I was trying to think what other mean things I could say, when my father came flying out of the living room with one of the newspapers rolled up in his hand. He hit me across the side of the head.

"Don't you ever let me hear you talk to your mother like that again," he said.

My ears rang and I felt tears. All three of us stood, not one of us knowing what to do or say. My mother slowly lifted her hands from the sink and dried them on her apron. She went to their bedroom and closed the door. My father's hand, which had been hovering in midair with the rolled-up newspaper, dropped. He let the paper fall to the floor, then he turned and left the house. I finished the dishes. We never spoke of the incident.

My mother's death was very hard on my father. She was killed when he fell asleep at the wheel one night and rolled the car on the highway just outside of Banff. They were coming back from visiting my Uncle Bob and his wife Elizabeth in Calgary. My father always had trouble staying awake when he was driving at night, but my mother never learned to drive so he couldn't hand the wheel over to her. I overheard somebody say at the funeral that my father had been drinking. He brought that up later, when we were alone.

"Don't you believe it," he said to me. "No matter what, don't you believe it. That's just the kind of rumour that dogs a person who's had more than the average dose of bad luck."

The funeral was in Saskatchewan, where my mother had grown up, and she was buried in a little country graveyard next to her parents, and a brother who had died in infancy. Her family, my aunts and uncles and cousins, still lived in the area and kept the graves up, placing new bouquets of plastic flowers in the little glass cups in front of the headstones every spring.

I wondered why he'd decided to bury her there. I wanted him to buy a plot, three plots, so we could all be buried together. He said he wouldn't know where to buy them. We'd moved too much, he said, and he didn't want to bury my mother in a place where nobody knew her.

"What about Banff?" I asked. "We like it there." I was thinking we would stay in Banff. I'd even heard my parents talk about trying to buy a house.

"This is better for your mother," he said, and we drove back to Banff, leaving her in the care of her relatives.

My father carried a tremendous amount of guilt and, as if his causing the accident wasn't enough to make him feel guilty forever, my mother had a fifty-thousand-dollar insurance policy, purchased through the company he worked for. I remember him sitting on the couch, staring at the cheque when it came.

"I don't want this, Meg," he said to me.

"Give it back then," I suggested.

"You can't do that," he said.

The cheque lay around the dining room table like a piece of mail too important to throw out but not important enough to do anything about, until I noticed one day it wasn't there anymore. I found out later that my father had put it in a trust account for me.

My mother died in February. At the end of April, my father lost his job. He was told insurance sales were down and the company was cutting back the number of agents on staff. He had been the last one hired, so he had to be the first to go. He said he didn't buy that. If they'd really liked his work, he said, they would have transferred him to another town.

"That dog turns you into a pariah," my father said. "Nobody wants you if he's hanging around showing his teeth. They're all afraid he'll turn on them someday."

That night he went out after supper and came home drunk. I'd never seen him drunk before. He called my Uncle Bob and tried to make him tell the truth about why he was fired. Uncle Bob told him the same thing he'd already been told.

My father started going out during the day. I didn't know where he went, but I sometimes saw him sitting on a bench in front of the King Eddy Hotel with two or three other men. When I did, I would put my head down and turn a corner, hoping he wouldn't see me and call out. He sometimes didn't come home for supper. At first, he would phone and tell me he wasn't coming, but then he stopped phoning. A month or so after he lost his job, our lives fell apart.

Two girls from school had asked me to go downtown for a milkshake with them. I didn't have many friends, because we moved so much I supposed, and I was hoping this was the beginning of something. I liked them. The three of us were walking down Banff Avenue toward one of the cafés when we saw a group of Hare Krishnas singing on the corner across the street. My father was with them. He was singing badly and juggling three cheap plastic balls.

"That's your father, isn't it," one of the girls said.

"You go ahead," I said to the girls. "I'll catch up with you in a minute."

"I didn't know your father was a Hare Krishna," the other girl said. They went on toward the café, looking back over their shoulders at me on one side of the street and my father on the other.

I watched as a police car pulled up and two officers got out. The

Hare Krishnas quit singing and moved down the sidewalk. I ran across the street.

"What are you doing?" I said, trying to grab my father's arm. He was still juggling the balls and singing. He ignored me. I could smell beer on him.

"Do you know this man?" one of the policemen asked me.

"He's my father," I said, tugging, trying to get him to drop the balls.

"You better take him on home," the policeman said. "I think maybe he's had a bit too much to drink. Make him a pot of coffee." He was trying to look stern but I could tell he thought my father was a joke.

"He hasn't been drinking," I said, finally succeeding in throwing him off so he dropped all three balls.

"Meg, Meg, Meg," my father said, looking at me now. The balls bounced, then rolled down the sidewalk.

"Come home," I demanded. "Come home with me right now."

He came without arguing.

"We should have gone to church," my father said on the way home. "We should have made you go to Sunday school."

"Mother was right," I said to him. "You are a fool."

When we got home, he lay down on the couch and fell asleep. When he woke up he called Uncle Bob again and tried once more to get him to say the insurance company fired him because they didn't want a loser hanging around, making everybody else's good luck turn sour. They argued on the phone, then my father started to cry. He dropped the receiver and let it dangle on its cord, and I heard Uncle Bob's voice telling him to pick it up. My father drooped forward in his chair until his head was down on his knees. I picked up the phone. Uncle Bob told me he was driving out from Calgary right away. My father was still sitting in the same chair when Uncle Bob got there an hour and a half later. I answered the door when he knocked, and he asked me if I would leave him and my father alone. I went to my room.

I thought about my mother. I tried to remember a time when we were really happy, the three of us. All I could remember were little scenes, like my mother and father laughing and writing silly postcards at Christmas time. Why wasn't there more? Why wasn't there a time when we were drenched in happiness, wet to the skin with our arms open, expecting more?

My father and Uncle Bob talked for over an hour, then I heard the front door and what I thought was Uncle Bob's car pulling away from the house. I heard footsteps in the hall, then a knock on my bedroom door.

"Come in," I said.

It was Uncle Bob.

"Your father wants you to come to Calgary," he said. "We talked about it and that's what he said. He thinks it would be best."

"I don't care what he thinks is best," I said, starting to cry. "It's best that I stay with him."

"It's not, Meg," Uncle Bob said. "Not right now."

I tried to tell Uncle Bob about the bad luck dog then, and how I was the one who could keep it at bay.

"Don't, Meg," he said, sitting beside me. "Don't do this to yourself. You're too young."

"That dog will eat him up," I said.

Uncle Bob pulled me to him.

"I love your dad," he said. "Just remember that I love your dad. He's my brother."

Uncle Bob stayed overnight with me, and we waited, but my father didn't come home. In the morning we packed my things and went to Calgary, where Aunt Elizabeth was waiting for us. I enrolled in the highschool close to their house, planning to finish my year and then move to wherever my father found a job. I thought about my mother often, about her relatives making sure she was looked after the same way my father's brother and his wife were looking after me. I tried not to think about my father travelling the highways and grid roads of the west with a mean dog snarling at his heels. I waited for the end of June and his arrival to pick me up and take me to wherever he was going. And when June passed I waited through July, and then August, and then it was September and another school year. Aunt Elizabeth bought me new clothes and paid for me to take dance lessons and driver training. In October a letter came from my father saying he hadn't found work yet. It was postmarked Yellowknife, Northwest Territories. I made a few friends at school and by Christmas I even had a boyfriend. I stopped waiting for my father to pick me up.

He did eventually call. He was working, managing the Co-op store in Cluny, Manitoba, and he phoned to ask me if I wanted to live with him again. But by that time I was into my final year of highschool and I didn't want to jeopardize my chances of getting into university by changing schools and maybe not getting as good grade twelve marks as I knew I'd get if I stayed in Calgary. I told him that, and he said he understood. Then he told me he'd met a woman. Coral was her name and they were thinking about getting married. I said I was happy for him. He told me Coral wanted to meet me, and suggested they pick me up after the school year ended and we'd go on a little holiday to the mountains. Coral had never been to the mountains. I said I would like that.

They picked me up on the last day of June. They were driving a nice car, pulling a tent trailer. Coral was quite a bit younger than my father, but that didn't bother me. She had a couple of magnetic game boards with her, and we played checkers or parcheesi in the back seat while my father drove. She had several books on plants and birds and rocks, and she kept them handy beside her. Sometimes she'd make my father stop the car while she looked something up. I liked her. I enjoyed the holiday and seeing my father again.

I remember most the day trip we made, at Coral's suggestion, to a secluded mountain lake near Lake Louise. In spite of the strenuous hike, there were tourists everywhere, cameras and binoculars around their necks. Many of them sat quietly in awe, resting on the huge boulders left by an ancient glacier in retreat. They had come, like we had, to marvel at the blue-green mountain water and study the ancient glacier, which still clung to the side of the mountain.

Coral picked up small chunks of rock and compared them to the pictures in one of her books, trying to determine what kind they were, selecting her favourites and stuffing them in her pockets. When my father saw her picking through the rocks, he became interested in them too. He chose several and weighed them in his hands, then held them up to the light as though studying the contours.

I sat on a big rock and watched Coral and my father and the tourists. A young man looking at the glacier shouted in Japanese, and his companion translated for everyone that he'd spied two climbers on the glacier. People trained their binoculars on the icy slope.

An older man was sitting on a rock near me. He sighted the climbers, then offered me his binoculars. I said, "No, thank you."

"I never thought I'd see a mountain climber," he said to me. "Did you?"

"No," I answered.

"You wouldn't catch me up there for anything," he said.

"No, me neither," I said.

With everyone watching the climbers, it was quiet all of a sudden, except for the birds. I could feel the space, the depth of the valley in which we were all sitting. I closed my eyes and listened to the birds. They were nutcrackers. Coral had already looked them up in her bird book.

"Well, would you look at that," the man next to me said.

I opened my eyes. The man was watching my father, who was on the shore of the lake, the glacier and the incredible blue-green water behind him. He was juggling rocks.

"Would you look at that," the man said again. The tourists began lowering their binoculars, poking the people next to them, and pretty soon all eyes were on my father.

Coral came and stood next to me.

"That's pretty good," she said. "I didn't know he could do that. Did you know he could do that?"

I nodded.

"Those rocks must be damned heavy," someone behind me said.

I didn't see rocks. I saw oranges. Rising and falling, briefly touching my father's hands, then rising again. I saw an old hound dog stretched out at his feet, resting, watching with lazy eyes. My father never missed a beat.

Safe House

W E MOVED into Bill Henkie's trailer after Carney found out the urea-formaldehyde insulation in our own house was going to kill us. We were living in an almost deserted town a twenty-minute drive from the city, and Bill's trailer sat on the lot next to ours. That was ten years ago, when I still thought there was a chance Carney would take advantage of Jimmy Carter's pardon and try to make some kind of amends with his parents, who live in Texas. What I really wanted him to do was take Meika and me to Texas and show us off. We were all the proof his parents would need, I thought, that he'd done well in Canada. Carney knew better. He showed me a letter in which his mother called him a coward and a communist, and told him he'd disappointed God and broken his father's heart.

"In my family," Carney said, "if you disappoint God and break your father's heart, you might as well be dead."

That was nothing I could relate to because my mother didn't believe in God and wanted to see more than just my father's heart broken. But I took Carney's word for it. He was older than me and seemed to know better about a lot of things.

After Carney found out how bad urea-formaldehyde foam was, he decided immediately to gut the house and reinsulate with a good eight inches of fibreglass. When I got up the next morning with Meika he was already pounding out the old lath and plaster walls in the living room. When I saw the plaster dust beginning to float from the living room to the kitchen and down the hall to the two small bedrooms, I asked Carney what Meika and I were supposed to do for the next however long this was going to take.

"Are we supposed to eat and sleep with paper dust masks on?" I asked.

"Don't worry, I'm ahead of you there," Carney said through his own safety mask. "We can move in with Bill."

"Move in with Bill?" I said. "You mean Bill next door? Bill Henkie and that damn dog?"

Carney knew Bill Henkie from the railroad. He was an electrician in the diesel shop and worked on the engines. Carney said he was one of those guys who had a special way with machines. All I knew about him was he was big and had a mean dog, a black lab. The dog was always tied to the back step of the trailer and barked viciously whenever I walked by with Meika in the stroller.

"You've got to be joking," I said.

"I caught him this morning before he left for work," Carney said, still working hunks of plaster off the wall with a mallet and crowbar. "No problem. You can cook for him once in a while. Clean up his trailer. Works out for all of us."

"Carney," I said, "I don't want to live with some old guy you know from the railroad. And what about that dog? He'll eat us for sure if we set foot near the place."

"The dog's all bark, and Bill's hardly ever home," Carney said. "You'll be lucky if you see him once a day. Besides, Bill's quiet as a mouse. He probably won't even talk to you. Women make him nervous."

I sat down with Meika on my knee. She grabbed at my earrings. Her diaper was wet and I tried to hold her so she wouldn't soak through onto my housecoat.

"I'd rather move into the city for awhile and stay with my mother," I said.

Carney stopped pounding and pulled down the dust mask. It cupped his Adam's apple.

"Hey babe," he said. "If you move in with your mother, I'll hardly ever see you."

It was true that my mother still wouldn't let Carney in her house, even though we'd been married for two months. It went back to my getting pregnant with Meika and Carney refusing to do the right thing and marry me. It wasn't that he didn't want me or the baby. He just didn't want to get married and he wasn't about to let my mother bully him into it. My mother had a hard time understanding his stance on the matter. Also, she had big problems with Carney because he wasn't a highschool teacher. She'd been telling me I should marry a teacher ever since she noticed that most of the cars in the teachers' parking lot at my highschool were practical, late models. That meant teachers made a good living and didn't squander it. They had down-to-earth aspirations, she theorized, that tended toward family life.

"Take a lawyer," she said to me once. "He'll go out and buy a Porsche as soon as he can afford it. Now a car like that is nothing more than an advertisement. 'I fool around on my wife,' is what a car like that says. You won't find many teachers driving around advertising their willingness to commit adultery. They're busy coaching little league and singing in choirs. And they know about things. History. How plants reproduce. Important things."

I tried to tell her that Mr. Caron who taught grade eleven and twelve English knew mostly about winking at girls and copping feels whenever he got the chance.

"You wish," she said. "Don't you just wish."

"He pinched my bum once," I said, but she wouldn't believe me and said my hormones were imagining things.

Carney was a major disappointment to my mother. For one thing, he was twelve years older than me, which would have been all right had he been a teacher, but he wasn't. He was a sculptor who made big abstract things out of machine parts and scrap metal. He owned a small run-down house in a dying town outside the city and made about minus five thousand dollars a year. I reminded my mother that he supplemented his negative income working off and on for the railroad, but that didn't appease her. And she didn't like the idea that he'd come to Canada as a draft dodger. She didn't like Americans, said they expected too much from life. I tried to explain to her that Carney didn't expect much at all, was quite happy to take things as they came, but that wasn't the right thing to say either so I gave up.

I was just out of highschool when I met Carney. At that time he was trying to make money teaching pottery classes and selling handmade bowls and mugs at craft fairs. I registered in a summer pottery class to keep myself busy because I couldn't find a job, and

Carney was the instructor. I used that later, the fact he was a teacher of sorts, but my mother didn't buy it. She said how to make mud harden in a brick oven was nothing anyone needed to know in the latter part of the twentieth century. And he drove an old Ford half-ton, which in no way fit her description of a vehicle that signified a family man. That was back before Carney started working for the railroad, when he still lived in the city in a one-room apartment with a bathroom down the hall.

My mother wanted me to take some kind of work-related course that fall, but I decided after the pottery class that I wanted to move in with Carney. We lived in his tiny apartment for a year, then he gave up trying to make a living as a potter and got the job working for the railroad as a spare labourer in the diesel shop. He bought the house twenty miles outside of the city for a thousand dollars and built a shed for his welding equipment in the back. He said he wasn't teaching any more two-bit classes or making any more damn pottery, and from now on it was the railroad for bread, and serious art for himself. Then I got pregnant and Carney put in the urea-formaldehyde foam to keep us warm and Meika was born and my mother announced she wouldn't have Carney in the house until he showed he was a man and married me.

When Meika was ten months old Carney gave in and we went to the doctor for blood tests. Carney asked two guys from the diesel shop to go to the courthouse with us to sign the papers, and a judge pronounced us man and wife while Meika crawled around in the Osh-Kosh overalls I got for her at the second hand children's clothing store. Afterward, we picked up a bottle of champagne to take to my mother's, but even though we held up the marriage licence for her to see, she wouldn't unhook the screen door as long as Carney was on the step. I pleaded. Meika started to cry because she wanted in.

"Piss on it then," Carney said and stomped down the sidewalk to the truck. My mother undid the hook.

I looked at Carney, and then at my mother, not knowing which way to go. Meika was leaning toward my mother, stretching to get out of my arms. Carney got tired of waiting for me to make up my mind and drove off.

"Come to Grandma," my mother said, opening the door and taking Meika. I went inside with the marriage licence and the champagne in the diaper bag. Later, when Meika was in bed and asleep, my mother did not object to drinking the champagne with me, although she refused to acknowledge it had anything to do with a wedding. In fact, she drank most of the bottle and I worried briefly that her capacity for alcohol seemed to have increased. I'd been noticing empty bottles on the counter lately, which she seemed to discard a little too quickly when she saw me looking at them.

After Carney left us at my mother's, he went out and got good and drunk with the two guys from the railroad. I stayed overnight with my mother and in the morning she noticed Meika had cradle cap on her scalp, and showed me how to use olive oil to prevent the yellow scales from forming. Carney pulled up out front late in the afternoon and honked the horn, and I packed up Meika and the diaper bag and got into the cab of the truck.

"What the hell happened to her?" Carney asked, looking at Meika's hair. "She looks like an ad for Brylcreem."

I told him she had undergone a home remedy to keep her from growing scales, and he snorted and we drove back to our little house, a legal family. I left the marriage licence on my mother's coffee table, hoping she would get used to having Carney for a son-in-law if she had a chance to study his name on her own time.

Carney had a terrible hangover. As soon as we got home he took a couple of 222s with codeine and went to bed. I would have crawled in with him, except Meika wasn't the least bit tired, so I entertained her with plastic baby toys and walked her around town in the stroller, the wheels catching on the gravelled streets. It was lonely in the empty town. There were more boarded-up houses than lived-in ones, and our own block was almost completely boarded up. I let Meika toddle around in a vacant lot for a while and finally she was ready to go to bed.

A few days later, the marriage licence arrived in the mail with a note from my mother. "I believe you left this by mistake," the note said. "It must be the case, because you should know by now it's nothing I'd be interested in having around."

Carney put his crowbar and mallet down in the plaster dust and poured himself a cup of coffee.

"So what do you say?" he asked. "Do I tell Bill it's a go?"

"I'm afraid of that dog," I said.

"The dog's all right. He's never bitten me," Carney said.

"I'll do it if you can guarantee the dog won't bite," I said. "You've got Meika here to consider."

"No problem," Carney said. "Just one other thing though. Bill's picky about keeping the trailer locked up. Says he's got some valuables he's worried about. That's why he's got the dog. He says we should lock the door whenever we go out. Even if it's just for a few minutes."

"But the town's practically deserted," I said. We never locked our doors, even if we were going to be gone for the whole day.

"I don't know," Carney said. "But that's the way he wants it."

We moved in the next day. We covered most of our furniture with plastic and moved only our bed and Meika's crib into Bill's extra bedroom. He'd been storing his work clothes in it, and even after I cleaned it up it still smelled of that mix of oil and dirt. The rest of the small trailer was filthy too, but Carney convinced me we'd only have to live there for a few weeks. There was no work for him in the diesel shop just then, and he said he'd be able to get up at the crack of dawn every morning and work on the house until ten or eleven every night.

Carney told Bill I was afraid of the dog, so Bill made Meika and me go through the ritual of being introduced. He said the dog wouldn't hurt us as long as he'd seen us going in and out of the trailer with him a few times. I held Meika tightly on my hip with one arm as Bill had me hold out my other hand for the dog to sniff.

"Don't be afraid of him," Bill said. "They can smell fear." That didn't make me feel any better, but the dog didn't growl at us anymore. From then on, we came and went and the dog paid hardly any attention to us. He'd lie for hours without moving from the bottom step, and we'd have to step over him if we wanted to go out. I started to feel sorry for him and bought him bones with the groceries. He began to look happier and I decided he barked a lot because he spent too much time alone.

I wanted to clean Bill's trailer top to bottom as soon as we moved in because it gave me the creeps, but Carney wanted me to hang around while he worked so I could take photographs of him and the inside of our house being torn apart.

"Can't I just come over at the end of the day and take a few pictures?" I asked.

He said I had to be there all the time to capture the whole process of tearing apart and putting back together. So while I stood around or tried to find a place to sit with Meika in the mess, Carney handed out orders for camera angles and shutter speeds and went on and on about how he was going to use the pictures in some art project. It started to get on my nerves. After three days of this, I snapped.

"The thing is," I said, "I thought you were supposed to be making our house safe and warm. Now you're working on an 'objet d'art' and meanwhile I'm living in a filthy trailer that belongs to somebody else. And I don't have time to clean it up because I'm spending all my time putting you in pictures."

"The thing is," Carney said, "There's no 'objet d'art' when you're working on a purely conceptual piece."

"I thought you were working on our house," I said.

Just then Meika fell on something and howled. Carney was quick to comfort her and gave me a look that said her hurting herself was my fault. I threw the camera at him and told him I was through taking pictures. I took Meika and went back to Bill's trailer.

That was the end of the art project, or at least that was all I heard about it. For a time I felt guilty. I didn't have to tell him I was through altogether. I could've gone over every hour or something. But in the end it didn't matter because Carney never did finish the renovations and his record of photographs would have been incomplete, even if I hadn't quit when I did.

Carney had been right that we would hardly ever see Bill. He left for work at five-thirty in the morning and didn't come home until well after midnight every night. And when I did see him, he hardly spoke. Introducing me to the dog seemed to have him left with nothing else to say.

The first morning we were there, I got up to make him his breakfast. I was standing at the stove in my housecoat, frying bacon and eggs in a grease-blackened pan, when Bill came into the kitchen tucking in his khaki work shirt and tightening his belt. He looked surprised to see me, even though he must have smelled the bacon cooking, then he quickly looked down. I could see his grey work socks were stiffly in need of washing.

"There's no need for you to do that," he said.

"It's the least I can do," I said.

"I usually have breakfast at the Esso on the highway," he said, sitting reluctantly at the place I had set for him.

I served him his breakfast and he ate it. I stood, embarrassed, and watched him eat, waiting to pour him coffee or fry him another egg. I felt like I was invading his privacy. Company, especially mine, obviously pained him and I wondered why he had even agreed to let us stay there.

"Perhaps I could make your lunch instead of breakfast," I said. I had noticed the black pail in the fridge, the thermos of hot coffee already made the night before and waiting on the counter.

"You could do that," he said. And from then on I made his lunch at night and put it in the fridge. I didn't know how much lunch he liked to eat, but I guessed a lot because he weighed about two hundred and forty pounds. I usually made him four whole sandwiches and threw in some muffins or a piece of pie and an apple, and he didn't ask me for more or less, so that must have been about right.

Bill's trailer had a kitchen and living room area, a bathroom, and the two bedrooms at the end of a narrow hallway. The bedroom walls were a kind of plastic panel board with little green flowers. I assumed the other bedroom, Bill's own, was exactly the same. I never looked inside, even when I was cleaning, because my mother had taught me to respect the privacy of bedrooms.

The trailer was set on a foundation of cindercrete block piles. The wooden porch, which also smelled of oil and dirt, was built around the outside door. It served as a place for the dog to sleep and as a storage shed for boxes of old comics and several hundred empty ice cream pails. The porch led to the kitchen and living room area, which had brown panel board on the walls and green indoor-outdoor carpet on the floor. Bill had a television set and an old green couch in the living room, and a battered chrome dinette suite in the kitchen area. That was about it for furniture. There were no curtains anywhere, except for dirty plastic shreds hanging in the bathroom.

The trailer shook when you walked down the hall. That's how I knew Bill was home every night. I felt the trailer shake as he walked down the hall to the bathroom, and then to his bedroom. It shook again as he rolled around, trying to settle in bed and go to sleep. He often rolled around for two hours or more, and some nights he didn't seem to sleep at all.

Except for that one encounter over breakfast, I had little to do with Bill. He was off work on Sundays, but when Sunday came I usually packed up Meika and drove into the city to my mother's for the afternoon, where we'd watch television or argue about Carney, and I'd try to count the number of drinks she was having. I stayed until nine or ten at night, and when I got home I said hello to Bill if he was around, then went to bed. During the week, I was always in bed at night before he got home. Sometimes Carney would stay up and talk to him, what about I had no idea, and I didn't ask. Once Carney and I were eating supper and he said, "Bill's okay. He's not everybody's cup of tea, but he's okay," and I didn't follow it up with a single question.

There was something that made me not want to know more about Bill than I already knew. Maybe it was the dirt in his trailer. Maybe it was his inability to sleep at night. Or his insistence that we lock the door whenever we left the trailer, even for a minute. I certainly wasn't afraid of him. If anything, I felt sorry for him. But the trailer told me as much as I wanted to know: he liked ice cream, he read comics, he stayed out late at night.

The other thing the trailer told me was that Bill had no interest in cleanliness. I couldn't live in it, even for a short time, the way it was. So after I freed myself up from taking pictures of Carney, I went out and bought two grocery bags of cleaning powders and liquids and brushes, and between rounds of keeping Meika fed and happy, I resigned myself to being a cleaning lady. When Bill noticed the difference, he thanked me politely and said the trailer hadn't looked that good since it was new. I was pleased with the compliment.

Even though the trailer was relatively comfortable after I got it cleaned up, I was still impatient for Carney to hurry and get the work done on our house. Bill's tossing and turning in the night bothered me, and the bedroom we were in was too small. Meika wasn't sleeping as well as she did at home, and she was so close to us and the trailer was so shaky that I felt self-conscious making love. Carney grew impatient about that, and I figured if anything was going to encourage him to hurry up and finish our house, it would be the damper on his sex life.

At first, Carney assured me it wouldn't be much longer, but then, after we'd been in Bill's trailer for a month, he told me the reconstructing part was going to cost more than he'd thought it would. He'd heard you could get a government grant to help you replace urea-formaldehyde insulation, but I told him I didn't want to wait for a government grant to come through. That could take ages.

"For Christ's sake, Carney," I said. "If we wait for a grant we'll be living with Bill forever. You shouldn't have started the job if you can't finish it."

"I didn't say I couldn't finish it," he said. "We're kind of running out of money. That's all."

"Kind of running out of money?" I said. "What does kind of mean? Are we or aren't we?"

"Well yeah," he said. "We are."

"Great," I said. "Great. I can't believe this."

Then Carney said, "Don't worry, babe," which was getting to be his favourite thing to say, and he phoned up his boss at the railroad and found out someone in the shop was taking sick leave. His boss told him he could get some work if he wanted, and he took it. So a few weeks of living in Bill's trailer stretched into six, and Carney was working much the same hours as Bill and sometimes he stayed out late to drink with the guys. I felt like Carney had gotten me into something I hadn't wanted in the first place, and then deserted me. I wondered if I should just pack up and move in with my mother, even if it meant I wouldn't be seeing much of Carney. I wasn't seeing much of him anyway.

My mother lived in a two-bedroom, 1950s bungalow in a working-class part of the city. My father had left her when I was a baby and she'd had no contact with him since. She'd more or less sworn off men the whole time I was growing up, except for half a dozen dates that had been arranged by her misguided friends. She came home early after every one of these dates, never invited her escort in, immediately fixed herself a stiff drink as though she'd been through hell, and generally made fun of the evening and the man for days after. She was downright cruel, I thought, although I was perfectly willing to join in and laugh about these men I had only glimpsed standing on our front step. There was Alvin, who sold shoes for a living, drove a sports car, and talked all night about how much his finger hurt because he'd slammed it in a car door two days earlier. And Peter, who'd taken her to an Italian restaurant and then slurped his spaghetti so he'd gotten tomato sauce all over the front of his shirt. And Max, who'd driven a long, lean Cadillac and laid on the horn at every red light. My mother's main criticism of these men was that none of them were what she would call "family men," men you could trust your life to. Really, though, I came to believe she didn't want any man around, and narrowing the definition of a good man only served to protect her from having to get married again. By the time I got to highschool she had told her friends to stop their matchmaking. That's why, when I went to visit one Sunday after Carney started working for the railroad again, I was surprised to find her having breakfast with a man.

"Oh," my mother said when she saw me standing on the front step with Meika reaching out to her. Her hair, usually pulled back into a ponytail or braid, was dishevelled and her make-up looked like last night's.

"Well. Come in," she said. "There's someone you should probably meet."

She took Meika from me and I followed her to the kitchen where she introduced me to Tony, who was sitting at the table. He stood and shook my hand vigorously.

"Tony manages a sporting goods store, don't you, Tony?" my mother said.

"Yes," said Tony, still standing. "We specialize in golf supplies."

His eyes looked a little bloodshot. My mother's did too. Were they having a torrid affair?

"And skates," my mother said. "He sharpens ice skates too. The good hockey players all come to Tony to get their skates sharpened. What's that team, Tony? The one that won the cup last year? Anyway, they all get Tony to sharpen their skates."

"It was just a minor league team," Tony said. "But yeah, they come to us. I guess they like the way we sharpen skates." He turned to Meika. "And who might this be?" he asked, reaching for Meika's hand. She pulled it away and looked at him suspiciously. She'd never seen a man in my mother's house, not even her own father.

"This is my granddaughter," my mother said. "Born out of wedlock, but they say they're married now."

"Mother!" I said.

"It's true, isn't it?"

I didn't bother to answer, but suddenly I noticed the vodka bottle on the breakfast table next to the orange juice container. Mother and Tony, it appeared, were both drunk.

Tony finished off what was left in his glass, then moved toward the door. "I have to get going," he said. "Meeting some people for a round of golf."

"I'll see you at supper time," my mother said.

"Yeah," Tony said. "Supper time. Should be here by five or six. Seven at the latest."

He stumbled, and I wondered how he could possibly make his way around a golf course.

"Nice to meet you," he said to me on his way out.

"Mother," I said after he was gone. "What in the world are you doing? That man is a drunk."

"He's not a drunk," she said. "He's a respectable businessman. He just likes his vodka and orange juice on Sunday morning."

"Then he's definitely a drunk," I said.

"Don't be smart with me," she said.

"How long has this been going on?" I asked.

"Eleven days," my mother said. "We haven't wasted any time, for reasons you wouldn't understand."

"Why didn't you tell me before?" I asked. "You could have told me last Sunday when I was here."

She set Meika down on the kitchen floor. Meika immediately toddled over to the lower cupboard and started pulling out canned goods.

"So what am I supposed to do?" my mother asked. "Am I supposed to sit around the house for the rest of my life watching television?" Her voice tightened like she was about to cry. I'd never seen my mother cry. "I'm forty-four years old," she said.

"Am I supposed to just sit here and rot? I deserve to have a little fun before I'm dead and buried."

"Is this fun?" I asked. "Getting soused on Sunday morning and then spending the day alone while Tony or whatever his name is goes out to play golf?"

"Don't lecture me," she said. "You know nothing. You know absolutely nothing about my life before you came along or since you decided to get yourself knocked up and married to someone who can't even earn a decent living."

"I think we had best not carry this conversation any further," I said.

"Perhaps we had best not," she said, and defiantly poured herself another drink. It was painful to watch her knock it back. It was like listening to Bill Henkie roll around in his bed every night, only she was my mother.

Meika screamed when I took her away from the cans of corn and tomatoes and green beans. When we were outside on the front step I shouted through the screen door at my mother.

"I'm sick and tired of you treating Carney like he doesn't even exist," I said. "Carney does a fine job of looking after me. Just as good as you did. So stop implying otherwise."

She didn't answer.

When I got back to the trailer, Carney and Bill were sitting on the couch drinking beer and watching a Clint Eastwood movie on TV. Two empty ice cream bowls were on the carpet in front of them. The dog was in the house, asleep under the table. He looked at me when I came in, then went back to sleep again.

"You're home early," Carney said. I stood with Meika asleep on my shoulder.

"Why aren't you working on the house?" I asked.

"Give a guy a break," Carney said. "Even God rested on Sunday."

"That's because He managed to get the work done," I said. "If He hadn't, He wouldn't have rested."

"Well, thank God He did," Carney said. "If He'd taken any longer we'd have a longer work week." By this time I'd seen the handgun sitting on the couch between them, and Carney saw me staring at it.

"Hey," he said. "This is incredible, it really is." He picked up the gun. "Don't worry. It's not loaded. Now this gun, this exact gun, is the one Hitler shot himself with. What do you think of that?"

"How many beer have you had?" I asked.

"It's true," he said. "It really is. Bill, tell her how you got the gun. Tell her."

Bill had been staring at the TV. He shrugged without looking up. "She's not interested in that," he said.

"Sure she is," Carney said. "Tell her."

"I bought it," Bill said. "From this guy."

"Tell her the whole story," Carney said. "It's great."

"You tell her," Bill said. "You can tell it better."

"Meika is heavy," I said to Carney. "Would you mind taking her?"

"Just a sec," Carney said. "Listen to this. It's great. Bill bought the gun from a guy who collects Nazi stuff. You've maybe heard about him. There was a thing on the news once. He lives west of here, near Swift Current someplace. He used to travel around to all the fairs with a little trailer and show his collection to people for fifty cents or seventy-five cents. Something like that. Not the gun though. He didn't travel with the gun because he was too afraid someone would steal it." Carney paused, sighting down the gun's barrel like a child with a toy. "So," he continued, "they were drinking one night, Bill and this guy with the collection, and the guy tells Bill he's thinking about getting rid of the gun, because his security isn't good enough. He kept it in a safe and had a couple of guard dogs, but still, with all these neo-Nazis around, he thought it wasn't safe to keep it. So Bill bought it from him. Right there. For a pile of money, Bill won't say how much. The guy threw in one of the dogs. That's how Bill got the dog."

Bill looked up with a shy grin on his face, but didn't say anything.

"Incredible," said Carney, carressing the gun. "I mean, you can actually hold in your hand the gun that Hitler shot himself with. And Eva Braun too, I imagine." He turned to Bill. "Did the guy say he shot Eva Braun with this gun?"

"He didn't say that. No. Just himself."

Carney held it out to me. "Here. Touch it if you want."

"I don't want to," I said.

Meika was heavy on my shoulder. My mother was a drunk. I had no desire to touch any gun, and I didn't believe for a minute the gun was Hitler's. It was obvious Bill had been suckered. He was pathetic and I was angry with Carney.

"I want to talk to you," I said to Carney. "In the bedroom."

"Oh oh," Carney said to Bill. "I must be in trouble."

Bill stared at the TV and Carney followed me down the hall, the trailer shaking as we walked.

"Tell her not to talk to anyone about the gun," Bill called after us. "I keep pretty quiet about it."

I laid Meika in her crib, then I started to cry. At first Carney thought I was crying about the gun being in the trailer.

"Don't worry about it," he said. "He doesn't even own bullets for it. He told me so."

That didn't stop me, so Carney decided I was crying because our house was taking so long and we had to live with Bill, and that *was* the reason, but not the whole reason.

"Look," he said. "Give me until Friday. I get paid on Friday, and then I'll quit and use the money to finish the house. Or at least finish it enough for us to move back in."

"That'll be just great," I said. "You expect Meika to crawl around with power tools all over, and nails and crowbars and God knows what else."

"Jesus babe, give me a break," he said. "I'm the doing the best I can."

Which was more or less true. So I resigned myself to a few more weeks of listening to Bill roll around in the next room half the night, and I tried not to think about my mother and Tony. The gun disappeared from the couch and went back, I assumed, to whatever hiding place Bill had for it. I didn't like the idea of a gun being in the trailer even if it wasn't loaded, but there was nothing I could do about it, and at least the end of our living there was now in sight.

As it turned out, the end of our living with Bill Henkie came sooner than I expected. Carney was supposed to be home for supper one night, but he phoned to say he was in the city and was staying for a few drinks. I knew what that meant so I went to bed. About midnight I heard someone come into the trailer and I didn't know whether it was Bill or Carney. I lay listening, trying to figure it out, when I heard what I was pretty sure was Bill moaning. There was silence for a while, then more moaning. I didn't know what to do. If Bill was drunk, I wanted to stay where I was and not have anything to do with him. On the other hand, if he was hurt I felt I should get up and try to help him.

The moaning continued and it didn't sound like drunken noises and finally I got up and put my housecoat on. I opened the bedroom door and peeked down the hall. I could see Bill sitting at the kitchen table with his head down. With the door open a crack, it sounded like he was saying, "Bad news, bad news." I tried to imagine what that meant. Had he been fired from his job? Had he been to the doctor and found out he had cancer? I closed the door, unable to think what I could say to him if I went out there. Then I thought of the awful possibility that the bad news had something to do with Carney, a drunken car accident. Once I had imagined this, I couldn't stand it. I had to go to the kitchen and be told that Carney was all right.

I opened the door again, quietly so I wouldn't wake up Meika, and I walked down the hall, fearful at what I might be told. I walked softly and Bill didn't hear me until I was standing by the kitchen table. He looked up. I knew immediately that he was drunk.

"Is everything all right?" I asked.

He stared at me like he'd never seen me before in his life.

"I heard you and I just wondered if everything was all right," I repeated.

"All right," he said, trying to fix his eyes on my face. His neck and shoulders struggled to hold his head steady, but they gave up and his head dropped to the table again. "Bad news, bad news," he muttered, then he moaned something that didn't make sense.

"I'll make some coffee," I said, not knowing what else I could do for him.

I was standing at the counter putting coffee in the aluminum pot when he got up from the table and his chair fell back against the wall. He stumbled across the small kitchen and stood next to me at the counter. His words were slurred, but I clearly understood what he was saying.

"I could rape you," he said, not angry, just drunken and matter-of-fact. "I could do it and no-one would ever know."

My hands started to shake. I thought about the gun and wondered where it was. I tried to tell myself he didn't mean it. I'd heard guys say things like that before when they were drunk. It was just booze talking.

He said it again, this time challenging me.

"Why would you want to do that?" I asked, trying to keep from showing fear.

"I didn't say I wanted to," he slurred. "I just said I could."

"I'm going to make this coffee," I said, placing the pot on the burner. "And I think you should have some."

"I could do it," he shouted at me then. "I could do it if I wanted to." Now his eyes were wild and he swayed back and forth, holding onto the counter for support. The dog began to bark at the door. I tried to think what I should do but my thoughts wouldn't come in order. I kept seeing the door as an escape, but I'd have to run to the bedroom for Meika and I didn't want to be trapped in the narrow hallway.

"I know you could," I said. "I believe you."

Then, just as suddenly as he'd grown angry, he softened and stumbled away toward the couch, where he collapsed. He closed his eyes and the moaning started again.

"Bad news," I heard, then something incomprehensible.

I stood by the stove, praying he would pass out.

The coffee started to boil and I quickly turned off the burner so it wouldn't make any noise. Whenever he was silent for a minute I'd think about sneaking down the hall for Meika, but just when I'd be about to take a step he'd open his eyes and look at me. Then he'd close them again and mutter some more drunken phrases with a *bad news* or two mixed in.

The telephone on the counter beside me rang. Bill's eyes opened. He stared at me as I answered.

"Hello," I said.

"Babe?" It was Carney. "What are you doing up?"

"Carney," I said. "Where are you?"

"I'm still in the city. The truck's fucked up. I think I'll stay in tonight and try to get it fixed in the morning."

"No," I shouted, then lowered my voice and tried to stay calm.

Bill was still staring at me, his eyes swollen, but focused. "Do something right now."

"Right now? It's the middle of the night."

"Right now, Carney. Borrow a car. Immediately."

Carney was silent for a few seconds.

"You sound strange," he said.

"Yes."

"Yes? What's that supposed to mean?"

"Very strange," I said.

More silence.

"Are you all right?"

"No."

"Can you talk?"

"No."

"Is it Bill?"

"Yes."

"Shit. Listen. He sometimes gets weird when he's drunk. Is he drunk?"

"Yes."

"Okay. Hang on, babe. I'll get a car and be right home. He won't hurt you. He's just weird. Can you hang on?"

"I think so. If things stay the same."

"Good."

I heard the receiver click and then the dial tone. I hung up the phone and stood there, hardly daring to breathe. Bill closed his eyes. He seemed to fall asleep, but still I didn't move. There was a clock above the stove and I watched the hands. I heard Meika fuss for a bit and then stop, and I listened to the clock ticking, and finally I heard a car pull into the yard. The dog started barking again.

The door opened and Carney came in. Bill heard him and opened his eyes. He struggled to sit up straight.

"So," Carney said, looking from me to Bill, casing the situation. "What are you up to, Bill?"

"Carney," Bill said. "Carney. Sit down. Have a drink."

"There's nothing left to drink, Bill," Carney said, sitting beside him. "You drank it all. Hell, the least you could have done was save some for me."

"Have a drink," Bill said. "Have one on me."

"Hey. Haven't you been listening? It's gone. You drank it all, buddy."

"Carney," I said. "Maybe you shouldn't talk to him like that."

Carney shook his head at me and then nodded toward the bedroom, indicating I should leave.

"Is that coffee perked?" he asked me as I started down the hall.

"Almost," I said. "Just turn it back on for a few minutes."

I closed our bedroom door, lifted Meika out of her crib and held her. She snuggled against my chest, wearing only a diaper, completely relaxed in sleep. I heard footsteps and Carney came into the bedroom.

"He's okay now," Carney said. "He just gets a bit crazy when he drinks."

"A bit crazy?" I said. "He talked about rape. He said he could rape me and no-one would ever know."

"You're kidding," Carney said.

"No, I'm not."

"That's booze for you," he said. "Some guys can't handle it."

"I want to leave, Carney," I said, trying not to sound hysterical. "He's got a gun somewhere. I want to leave right now."

"He's just about out," Carney said. "In the morning he won't remember a thing."

"I don't want to sleep here tonight," I said.

"Go to bed," Carney said. "Nothing's going to happen. I'll sit up and talk to him until he passes out."

"Why won't you leave?" I asked. "Why can't we just leave now?"

"Shhhh," he said. "You'll wake up Meika."

He went back down the hall, closing the bedroom door after himself. I stood for a while, then I put Meika into our bed and crawled in beside her, still in my housecoat. I lay there, listening to Carney's voice coming from down the hall. Every once in a while I'd hear Bill laugh.

I wasn't asleep. I was somewhere in between asleep and awake when the bedroom door opened and Bill staggered in and tried to get into our bed. I screamed, grabbing Meika and pulling her toward the wall so Bill wouldn't fall on top of her. He got on his hands and knees on the bed and pawed at the blankets. Carney flew into the room and flipped the light switch.

"Jesus Christ, Bill," he said as he tried to drag him off the bed. "What the fuck are you doing now? This is my wife, for fuck sake. You can't get into bed with my wife."

I picked up Meika, who was now awake and crying, and crawled off the foot of the bed with her.

"I thought he'd gone to the fucking bathroom," Carney said, still struggling with Bill. Bill lashed out at him and knocked him against the wall.

I ran down the hall. One of Meika's baby blankets was draped over a kitchen chair. I grabbed it, wrapped it around her and ran outside, almost tripping on the dog. A white Chev sedan was parked by the trailer, the car Carney had borrowed. I got in on the passenger side with Meika and locked the doors. I held her for a minute, comforting her, then I reached over and started honking the horn. I honked until Carney came out of the trailer. I opened the driver's side for him and he got in and started the car. Someone away down the mostly boarded-up street switched a yard light on. Carney backed the car out of Bill's lot and headed toward the city.

"Where should we go?" he asked. I noticed his eye was swelling where Bill had hit him.

"My mother's," I said.

"A hotel," he said. "That might be better."

"I'm not going to a hotel," I said. "I'm going to my mother's."

We drove in silence the rest of the way. I was thinking how Carney must have known Bill was crazy, must have seen him in that shape before. He pulled up in front of my mother's house and turned off the car.

"He wouldn't have used the gun," Carney said. "Don't worry about that, if that's what you're thinking."

I opened the car door. "You don't know that," I said. "So don't pretend you do."

"He's just a bit crazy, that's all."

"You don't fuck with crazy people," I said.

Carney laid his head back against the headrest. The interior light was on because I was still holding the car door open. He shielded his eyes with one hand. I wanted him to say, "I'm sorry," and he did.

I wondered all of a sudden what his mother would do if she were here and he was saying sorry to her. And then I thought that

I wasn't like his mother. I was like my mother and I didn't care if he disappointed God. I just wanted him to care that we were safe.

I got out of the car with Meika, who was still asleep.

"Are you coming?" I asked Carney.

"She won't let me in."

"I'm tired of that nonsense," I said. "Come on."

I rang the doorbell while Carney stood behind me on the bottom step. The porch light came on and my mother answered.

"We need a place to sleep," I said. "And don't you dare tell Carney he has to go somewhere else. If you do, I'll never come home again."

Meika woke up and rubbed her eyes. My mother studied the three of us through the screen, then she unhooked the door.

"Come to Grandma," she said to Meika, reaching for her.

Dianne Warren

Dianne Warren is a fiction writer and playwright. Her plays "Serpent in the Night Sky" and "Club Chernobyl" were both produced at Saskatoon's Twenty-Fifth Street Theatre, and *Serpent in the Night Sky* was a finalist for the Governor-General's Award for Drama in 1992. She also won the Western Magazine Award for Fiction in the same year. *Bad Luck Dog* is her second collection of short fiction. Her first collection, *The Wednesday Flower Man*, was published by Coteau Books in 1987. She lives in Regina, where she is currently at work on a new play and a novel.

Richard Gorenko

Richard Gorenko is an artist living and working in Saskatchewan. His works are represented in many private and public collections throughout North America.